TRACES OF THE PAST

A Milo Forbes Mystery

Steve Laracy

MILFORD
HOUSE

Milford House Press

MECHANICSBURG, PENNSYLVANIA

MILFORD HOUSE

an imprint of Sunbury Press, Inc.
Mechanicsburg, PA USA

For information about special discounts for bulk purchases, please contact Sunbury Press Orders Dept. at (855) 338-8359 or orders@sunburypress.com.

To request one of our authors for speaking engagements or book signings, please contact Sunbury Press Publicity Dept. at publicity@sunburypress.com.

ISBN: 978-1-62006-065-0 (Trade paperback)

Library of Congress Control Number: 2019938283

FIRST MILFORD HOUSE PRESS EDITION: April 2019

Product of the United States of America
0 1 1 2 3 5 8 13 21 34 55

Set in Bookman Old Style
Designed by Chris Fenwick
Cover by Chris Fenwick
Edited by Chris Fenwick

Continue the Enlightenment!

To Peter, Tom, and Don -

for helping me survive the California Years

CHAPTER 1

OUT OF SAN DIEGO

I
f you drive west out of San Diego on Route 8, long after the
breeze off the ocean dies and the salty smell of the water is
replaced—or smothered—by the dust you inhale, you will
come upon a one-lane road on the left about halfway between El
Centro and Yuma. There is no sign indicating the road's name;
however, there is a weathered marker on a rusty metal pole which
reads *Bell City—50 Miles*. Turn left and follow the arrow on the
sign, and you will travel through open range interrupted by a few,
dusty towns until, after about thirty miles, you reach a smaller,
dustier town named Cordoba.

They say a dry climate is beneficial to your health. If that is
true, judging by the lack of vegetation and the abundance of dirt
and dust blowing around and covering everything that wasn't
moving (and a few things that *were* moving, like me), then Cordoba must be one of the healthiest places on earth. But I did not
go to Cordoba for the climate. Rather, I had an urge to leave San
Diego behind for a day and visit an old friend.

I became a resident of San Diego courtesy of a formal invitation
from the U.S. Navy. This invitation, called a draft notice, informed
me that my freedom was in peril if I declined to accept the gener-
ous offer extended by the government of the United States. I
accepted, and four years later, looking for employment after my
discharge, I discovered with disbelief that my qualifications as a
boatswain's mate did not translate well in the civilian market-
place. The duties of a boatswain's mate, as every sailor knows,
consist of three primary functions: If it moves, salute it; if it
doesn't move, move it; if you can't move it, paint it.

Having decided my qualifications were limited for any line of
work, I opened a practice as a private investigator in a

nondescript office in an undesirable neighborhood.

When I say I am a private investigator, my personality and experiences are not to be confused with private investigators you may be familiar with from books or movies. I will never be mistaken for Lew Archer or even Miles Archer. I am not much of a fighter and even less of a lover. Unlike Lew, I have never been punched in the face, and unlike Sam Spade's partner, I have never ended up dead in a San Francisco alley. I cannot even favorably compare myself to the actress Anne Archer, who, in the movies, sometimes got her man.

My practice has been limited to responding to wrong numbers, playing solitaire, and occasionally following a husband or wife suspected of infidelity. Most of my time is spent slouched down in my car with a cup of coffee, a Kodak, and a Snickers bar.

Deciding to get away for a day, I went to Cordoba to connect with an old friend from my Navy days, Ben Nye. Ben was now the mayor of Cordoba, and he had invited me for a visit to catch up on old times. Having somehow lost the six of hearts from my solitaire deck, I thought the timing was right to accept the invitation.

Beside the main road that enters Cordoba from the south—the road previously described—you'd notice a small, wooden sign which at one time read *Cordoba—Pop. 73*. The "*73*" had been crossed out by a knife and replaced with the words *goes the weasel*. A street sign notified visitors they were now traveling on Main Street.

The commercial district of Cordoba consists of several small businesses, three of which surround the main intersection of Main and Third. The general store sat on the southwest corner. Across Third Street from the general store, there is a tiny gas station. On the opposite side of Main Street and a few doors down from the general store, there's one of those old-fashioned metal diners shaped like a railroad car.

I made my first stop in Cordoba at the gas station. My visit was necessitated by a small boulder disguised as a big rock that attacked the undercarriage of my car as I approached the town. The damage required me to wobble my way into the gas station with minimal haste.

No one was in sight when I pulled in. In case someone was

watching from inside the station, I got out and stooped and looked at the underside of the car on the driver's side, trying to look like I knew what I was looking at, which I didn't. No one appeared, so I looked the place over. The store was a rundown wooden shack with a sign above the door that read *Hector's Gas Station and Bait Shop.* Out front was one old gas pump. When I say old, I determined this not just by its ancient appearance but because, rather than listing several octane grades, it offered only two choices—leaded or unleaded.

Still, no one appeared, so I headed for the shack. I thought of peering through the window to see if anyone was in, but alternate layers of dirt, grime, and dust eliminated that possibility. Instead, I went straight for the door. A bell attached to the inside top of the door announced my arrival and wakened a slight man who looked to be in his twenties. He had been sleeping in a plastic and aluminum lawn chair in a corner of the shop.

After shaking the cobwebs away caused both by the sleep and the lack of sanitary maintenance applied to the room, the man said, "Hi, what can I do for you, gas or worms?"

"Neither. I ran over a rock on the way into town and damaged my car. Are you Hector?"

"Hector Suarez, that's me," he replied, followed by, "I better take a look at the car,
Mr.—"

"Forbes, Milo Forbes."

Hector Suarez was a man of medium height but exceedingly thin. His appearance and speech suggested he was a Mexican American. He had a friendly grin and manner and a handsome, if thin, face marred only by the condition of his teeth (or rather, lack of teeth) exposed by his smile. Whether he lost half his teeth to poor care, disease, or fisticuffs, I have no way of knowing.

"I'll look at your car and be back in a minute, Mr. Forbes."

He stretched slowly and, just as slowly, left the shop and sauntered outside. Having nothing better to do, I surveyed my surroundings.

The shop was empty except for the lawn chair, a long, folding card table to the right which was used as a countertop, a battered cardboard box to the right of the counter, and an empty cigarette

machine to the left, which, in older and better times, had vended
Camels, Luckys, and Chesterfields for thirty-five cents. The floorboards were crude wooden slats spread across the ground with
the dirt below showing between the boards.

I walked over and looked inside the cardboard box. Inside was
a layer of dirt which was almost completely covered with earthworms. Having no mind to explore this further, I returned outside
to check on Hector's progress. However, as I turned, the bell on
the door announced his return.

"Looks like you bent the front axle," he offered.

"Can you straighten it?"

"Not me, Mr. Forbes. I'm not qualified to work on foreign cars."

"It's a Buick!"

"Doesn't matter," Hector replied. "I don't know nothing about
domestic cars either or any other kind."

"Where do I go from here?" I asked with a sinking feeling.

"I can call over to Bell City and have the car towed. There's a
garage over there that can handle the repairs."

"Any idea how long that will take?"

"I can get it towed this afternoon, but it will take a few days to
fix it."

"I guess that will have to do. Is there any place I can get a room
in town, and can you tell me where I can find Ben Nye?"

"I saw Ben heading to the diner a little while ago," Hector answered my last question first, "and there's a boardinghouse on
Fourth Street."

"Thanks. I see you sell worms. Is there any place to fish around
here?"

"There's a reservoir northeast of here but it's quite a drive."

"So, I guess you don't sell many worms?" I reasoned.

"Not many. The worms just crawl up through the spaces between the floorboards. I don't like killing them, so I figured I
would sell them instead. Mrs. C—that's Mrs. Cavendish—over on
Fifth Avenue has barn swallows living in the roof of her house and
buys worms from time to time."

"Fifth Avenue?"

"Yeah, there's only five streets off Main Street. Used to be
named First Street to Fifth Street, but when Mrs. C moved into a

big house on Fifth Street, she made the Mayor change the name to Fifth Avenue. She's a rich lady from San Francisco and sort of runs the town."

"The squeaky wheel gets the grease," I replied.

"Don't worry," Hector came back. "They'll grease your wheels when they fix the axle."

Rather than try to explain, I moved on.

"That explains the worms, but if you don't mind my asking, how does someone who knows nothing about cars end up owning a service station and selling bait in the middle of the desert?"

"Well, Mr. Forbes, I don't have much education, so there wasn't much else I could do. Also, I had a little trouble with the immigration people, so I figured I would be better off at an out-of-the-way place like this."

"Immigration trouble?"

"Yes, I got caught trying to sneak across the border at Mexicali and they sent me back."

"If they sent you back, how are you still here?"

"I'm a United States citizen, born in Tucson. The Mexican police shipped me back."

Confused, I asked, "You mean you tried to sneak *into* Mexico from the United States?"

"Sure. I wasn't making out too well here, so I thought my luck might change down there. Besides, there's a lot less traffic going that way, so I figured it would be easier."

"I hope you didn't get into too much trouble."

"No, the police down there treated me good while I was there, though the local police captain spent most of the time complaining about the lack of border security and wondering why the President of Mexico doesn't do more to stop the flow of illegal immigrants."

Deciding not to press my luck by asking another question, I said good-bye and, still reeling from my conversation with Hector, wandered out to clear my brain and find Ben Nye. I grabbed my suit jacket from the car, loosened my tie, and walked in the direction of the diner I had passed on the way in. I needed a cup of coffee by this time. I would then search out the boardinghouse and see about a room.

As I approached the intersection, a dusty bus drove by, headed south toward Route 8. I'm not sure whether the bus came from Bell City or somewhere farther north, but I had half a notion to leave the car and hop on the next bus, hoping it was headed toward the coast. If I had known then what I know now about the events that would occur in Cordoba over the next few days, I might have left and never looked back.

But then I would not have gotten to know the residents of Cordoba, most of whom I became fond of—and one in particular, I liked a lot. Some of the residents were strange and some had secrets, and each, like Hector, had a story to tell.

And if I had caught the next Greyhound out of town, I wouldn't have a story to tell.

CHAPTER 2

THE CORDOBA DINER

The diner was across Main Street and about half a block down in the direction from which I had entered town.

The Cordoba Diner is the type you see back East, shaped like a silver railroad car. This one was sitting on wooden blocks positioned on both ends, and it had a large, rusty tank attached to the back to hold water or fuel of some sort.

I had arrived in Cordoba around noon, and the heat and dust were affecting me by the time I made my way to the diner. The large yellow sun surrounded by the clear blue sky brought to mind a painting of sunflowers by van Gogh or some other painter I had seen in a museum in San Diego some time ago. I climbed the wooden steps and entered the Cordoba Diner, which welcomed customers with a hand-printed sign attached to the front door by double-sided tape.

After my eyesight adjusted from the bright afternoon light to the dim light inside, I looked around the diner. The interior would be familiar to anyone who has been in one of these boxcar-like diners. Straight ahead was a long, Formica-topped counter fronted by about ten or twelve swivel stools upholstered with bright-red plastic. The degree to which each stool had been occupied in the preceding years was determinable by the number of cracks in the plastic seat covers and the white stuffing peeking from between the cracks. I'm not sure what the inner material was made of, but it had the color and consistency of asbestos, which, for health reasons, I hoped it wasn't.

Behind the counter was an opening used to communicate with the kitchen to the rear and a door to the left to enter the kitchen. To the right was a little passageway that led to the restrooms. The rest of the back wall held shelves that contained the customary bowls of bananas, oranges, and grapefruit and tiny, individual boxes of cereal. The counter was populated with several sugar and salt-and-pepper shakers, napkin holders, and one glass-covered cake holder displaying what looked to be a carrot or spice cake. On closer inspection, I discovered this was a carrot cake, as evidenced by the little plastic carrots stuck on top of the white frosting. Also attached to the countertop were a few of those metal jukebox selectors with pages of selections that were flipped by a lever on the bottom.

Stretching across the front of the diner, facing Main Street and on either side of the entrance, were several booths. I will not describe the booths, other than to mention there was more Formica, red plastic, shakers, and napkins. To the far left was the vintage jukebox, filled with a collection of 45 records destined to be forever picked up, rotated, placed on a turntable, and played at the whim of the customers. Opposite the jukebox, at the right end of the diner, was a large oscillating fan on a stand. Conspicuously absent was an air conditioner, although, in my estimation, the furious spinning and turning of the fan was successful in keeping the temperature of the air inside the diner in the upper eighties.

I then turned my attention to the people present, of whom there were three. Two middle-aged men were sitting at the counter to the left, the closest of whom I recognized as Ben Nye. Behind the counter was a tall, ample woman, maybe late sixties or early seventies, with blonde, curly hair, either dyed or a wig.

Ben turned and studied me for a minute, recognized me, and jumped from the stool to come over and shake my hand.

"Milo, old friend," he exclaimed, "finally took up my invitation to visit!"

"Hello, Ben. Good to see you again. I decided I had postponed my visit for too long."

Ben now gave me a hearty slap on the back. "Well, it's about time!" he shouted. "I'd almost given up hope."

Ben had that familiar but strange look of a friend you haven't seen in years. I could tell that the features I remembered were tucked away inside his face, but they were somewhat distorted by the film of age. He was still tall and thin but a little more stooped.

His face had a healthy glow, and he still had a full head of black hair, although some white was working its way up his sideburns.

"Come in and have a cool drink," he continued. "You must be thirsty after your drive. Hilda, get my friend here a glass of iced tea." The last remark was directed to the woman behind the counter, who seemed to take a moment to digest the command and then to reluctantly take steps to comply with it.

"I think I'll have a black coffee and a glass of water," I said. I needed a quick jolt of java to keep me functional.

Hilda processed this second request at about the same speed and then glared at both Ben and me in succession. The menacing gesture was quickly replaced by a huge smile. "Come on over and sit down," she said, gesturing with her arm to a seat at the counter. "I'll get your drinks."

"Yes, come sit," Ben said, taking my elbow and leading me to the counter. He moved a half-eaten piece of cake and glass of milk from his place at the counter one spot to the right and seated me in between himself and the gentleman on his left, who was about halfway through a grilled cheese sandwich.

Ben introduced. "Milo, this is Phil Childers. He owns the general store across the street. Phil, this is my old Navy pal, Milo Forbes."

"Pleased to meet you, Milo," Phil offered.

"Hello, Phil," I replied, and then, to lighten the mood, asked, "Who's minding the store?"

Not catching my tone, Phil responded, "A young girl down the street watches things while I spend my time relaxing over here, chewing the fat with Ben."

"Milo is a private detective in San Diego," Ben informed Phil.

"Is that so?" Phil responded. Phil was a short, round fellow who was wearing a short-sleeve white shirt under a checkered vest. His face was as round as his body, and he had large, round brown eyes. Overall, he resembled a child's drawing of a human body made up entirely of circles. He had brown hair with a slight curl in the front, the hairline suffering from a reverse case of male pattern baldness: hair on the top of his head, bald on the sides. With his short stature, unusual hairstyle, and checkered vest, he would have fit right in as a resident of Munchkin Land.

After I had updated Ben and Phil on my car problems, Ben and I spent time reminiscing and updating each other on our lives, he as mayor of a small town, me as a big-town private detective, while I drank my coffee. When we had caught up, Phil jumped into the conversation.

"Say, maybe you can help with the little mystery we've been having. Couldn't hurt to have a professional opinion."

"Milo's just here for a short personal visit," said Ben. "I doubt if he's interested—"

"I don't mind if you'd like me to help," I interrupted. I was somewhat flattered that anyone would want my "professional opinion". Besides, I needed something to keep me busy for the next few days, and Cordoba didn't seem to offer much in the way of entertainment.

"Great!" said Phil. "You see, it seems someone has been snooping around the diner and the tavern, trying to break in. Hilda lives in the house out back and has seen a shadowy figure wandering around and peering through the windows of the diner and tavern late at night. The Flagg sisters down the hill have also seen him. Now in a big city that may not seem strange, but here in Cordoba there's not much crime, and there is nobody on the street after nine p.m."

Ben took up the story from there. "Nothing has been stolen or damaged as best we can tell, but it makes people nervous to know there's a prowler about. The positive side is it gives the ladies something to gossip about."

"Well, let me ask a few questions," I said, using my best PI voice. "First off, is there anyone new in town, say just moved here or visiting for a while?"

"No new residents," Ben replied. "And the only visitors are two fellows who showed up a couple weeks ago. One's a lightning rod salesman. I don't know what the other fellow does, but he tends to keep to himself. They're both staying over at the boardinghouse down the street."

"Did they arrive together?" I asked.

Phil answered this one. "They arrived separately but about the same time."

"Two weeks seems like a long time for a salesman to stay in a small town like this," I offered.

"He travels to Bell City and other towns in the area, plus he says the dry climate is good for his arthritis," Phil said.

"Okay, it looks like I'll be spending time at the boardinghouse myself, so I'll see what I can find out," I said. "The second question I have is: Where's the tavern? You say Hilda has seen the prowler hanging around the diner and the tavern from her house out back. But coming in I didn't see a bar in the neighborhood."

Ben laughed. "You're sitting in the tavern," he said. He then clarified his remarks.

It seemed the diner was owned jointly by Hilda Bluff and a man named Frank Blaine, who also lived in the house behind the diner. Hilda owned the daytime rights and operated the diner from 6 a.m. to 5:30 p.m. At 6 p.m. Frank took over, and the place became the Cordoba Tavern, where the locals gathered for a beer. This seemed like a strange arrangement and I had a few more questions about the relationship between Hilda Bluff and Frank Blaine, but they could wait. There were a few hours to kill before the tavern opened, and I wanted to check out the town of Cordoba and visit a certain lightning rod salesman. After a little more time spent lying about the old times with Ben, I got up to head back into the heat.

As I was leaving, Ben said, "Since you're stuck here for a few days, maybe you'd like to come with us over to the Tri-County Fair in Chiquita tomorrow. There's rides and lots of food, and you can meet some of the locals."

"Maybe I will," I said. A county fair in the middle of the desert seemed like just my cup of tea.

I hate tea.

CHAPTER 3

A STROLL AROUND TOWN

W hen I hit the street, the heat hit me back. I took a minute to recover and get my bearings. I walked across the street to buy a pack of gum at the general store. As I was about to enter, a girl of about nine or ten came out of the store.

"The store is closed for lunch, but if you need something you can get it and leave some money on the counter," she said. As she spoke, she was munching on peanuts from a little cellophane bag. I decided that she must be the girl Phil had mentioned.

"Isn't it risky leaving the store unattended," I asked, "with a prowler wandering around?"

"Nah," she responded. "He never takes anything, and he is only seen at night."

"How do you know it's a 'he'?" I was confident that my detective skills had impressed the girl.

"I guess I don't," she replied, unfazed. "But I've seen the footprints left around the back of the diner, and they seem too big to belong to a lady. I eliminated Miss Bluff's and Mr. Blaine's footprints, and nobody else has a reason to be back there. And research says that most prowling and break-ins are done by males. Still, I guess you caught me."

Suddenly I didn't feel so brilliant. I changed the subject and asked directions to the boardinghouse. The girl mentioned that she was going home for lunch and that the boardinghouse was in the same direction, so I walked along with her. As we walked, she did most of the talking.

The girl's name was Samantha Fremont. She had bright red hair and a smattering of freckles, was nine years old and lived on

Fourth Street with her parents, Bert and Millie, and her younger brother, Skipper. The boardinghouse was also on Fourth Street on the other side of Main Street and was owned and operated by Samantha's aunt, Felicity Fremont. Samantha, or Sam, as she preferred to be called, worked at the general store during the summer, and Mr. Childers paid her with a bag of peanuts while he took his break at the diner.

"You could say that I work for peanuts," she joked.

I told her I was a private investigator and a friend of Ben Nye's, and he had asked me to investigate the strange happenings at the diner.

"I can help you!" Samantha exclaimed. "Please let me help. My dream is to be a private investigator. My name is Samantha, but everybody calls me Sam because I want to be like Sam Spade."

"That explains your earlier observations, but I work alone."

"Please, please, please! I can do your legwork. And you don't have to pay me. And I know everybody in town, so I can hang around and talk to everyone without being suspicious."

"Well, okay," I gave in. I could use someone to run errands, and I could pick her brains concerning the citizens of Cordoba. Besides, she seemed bright for a nine-year-old.

We had reached the boardinghouse, which was an old Victorian building with a porch that extended all around the building. Sam led me up the steps, across the porch, and into the hall of the house. The hall had double doors on each side, the left leading to a dining room and the right into a parlor. Straight ahead was a stairway leading to the second floor. To the left of the stairway was a passage that that led to the kitchen. This was our destination since the proprietor was in the kitchen preparing lunch. Felicity looked up as I walked in with Samantha and said, "You must be Milo." She wiped her hand on a dishtowel and extended it toward me.

I shook her hand and said, "Word travels fast around here."

"Ben called from the diner and said you were on your way."

"I guess Ben didn't want me to surprise you."

Sam said, "My dad says the three fastest forms of communication in Cordoba are telephone, telegraph, and tell Mayor Nye."

Felicity and I both laughed. Sam told Felicity about our

discussion on the way over to the boardinghouse, so I took the opportunity to check out Felicity.

She was pretty with light-red hair, almost blonde, I guess what they call a strawberry blonde. Her face was oval-shaped, with a small, upturned nose, and green eyes, and looked to be in her late thirties, early forties. She was wearing a housedress and an apron but had a classy look and was easy on the eyes.

As I stared, I could see she was half listening to Sam while giving me a quick once-over at the same time. I had a few years on her, and my physique isn't what it used to be, but she didn't turn away in disgust.

"Will you be staying awhile?" Felicity asked. I hoped that she hoped I was.

"Well, the visit was planned as a day trip, but car troubles may keep me here for a few days."

"We'll take good care of you while you're here," Felicity responded. Although I wouldn't mind spending time with her, I wasn't looking forward to an extended stay in a backwater town like Cordoba.

"Mr. Forbes is a private detective, just like I want to be," said Sam. "He's investigating the happenings at the diner. "

"I think that may be more the Flagg sisters' imaginations than anything else." Felicity laughed. "There's not much crime around here. I would think this would be a dull place for a man like you."

I had to agree with that, although investigating a prowler was no less exciting than most of my experiences in San Diego.

"Mr. Forbes and I want to investigate your guests since they are the only strangers in town, don't we, Mr. Forbes?" Sam continued. "I'm Mr. Forbes's assistant, aren't I, Mr. Forbes?"

"I think you should let me do the talking, Sam. And since you're my assistant, why don't you call me Milo."

Felicity frowned, "I don't know that I approve of spying on my guests. They seem respectable, although Mr. Costello seems a little mysterious. I'm sure they would not be involved in criminal activities."

"I don't want to spy on them," I replied. "I just want to ask a few questions."

"Well, if that's the case, you'll want to stay for lunch. Mr. Costello is seldom late when meals are served," Felicity responded with a wink.

"Can I stay too, Aunt Felicity?" asked Sam. "Mr. For—Milo— might need me to take notes."

"All right, Dick Tracy," Felicity laughed, "but run home and tell your mother you're eating over here."

The last instruction was unnecessary as Sam was already out the kitchen door and halfway across the hall.

CHAPTER 4

LUNCHTIME

“ I prepared a simple lunch—salad and cold chicken,” said Felicity as we sat at the table in the dining room. The room was cooled by a couple of ceiling fans on either side of the long rectangular table. “Not like a fancy restaurant in San Diego.”

“A normal San Diego lunch, at least for me, comes in a sack and is ordered through the mouth of a large clown,” I said. “This will do just fine.”

Mr. Carmine Costello, who had already been seated at the table when we entered with the food, and to whom I had just been introduced, laughed at the last remark. He was a large, corpulent fellow with slicked-back black hair and a five o’clock shadow, sort of like Fred Flintstone’s. He had a small scar on his left cheek and looked like a man you wouldn’t want to cross.

“I agree with Mr. Forbes,” he said. “In my line, frequently traveling, you eat in many places, but not many as fine as yours, Felicity.”

“Thank you for the compliment, Mr. Costello,” Felicity said. “We don’t have any fast-food places in Cordoba. It’s the diner or the home. We may seem behind the times, but we like it that way.”

“Just what is your line, Costello?” I asked.

“A detective is never off duty,” he chided me. “I’d rather not discuss it right now, but perhaps at a later time we can have a talk.” He gave me a sinister smile.

Also at the table were Sam and Silas Collins, the lightning rod salesman, who had been eating with his head down and hadn’t spoken since the meal began. He was thin and his face was weather-beaten, so it was difficult to determine how old he was.

Sam, sensing a chance to join the investigation, said to Collins, "It must be interesting being a traveling salesman. You get to go to so many interesting places, I bet."

"Not so many, child," he responded. "I spend a good deal of time in motel rooms."

I could have used my vast knowledge of lightning rods to flush him out, but I had no such knowledge, so I said, "I didn't know there was much lightning in the desert."

"It comes in spurts," he said. "Out in the desert, it's called monsoon. Mostly stays high up and just puts on a little fireworks display, but every so often it spots a tree or a house or even a person that gives off a certain vibration, and then it takes aim."

"You speak of lightning as if it could think and make decisions on where to strike," said Felicity.

"Oh, it don't have a brain, per se," said Collins, "and it ain't really thinking, but still it attacks with a method. Maybe it's electrical currents, or maybe something more sinister, but it has a plan.

"I can always tell, by sight and smell, which houses need a lightning rod. It's a gift, or maybe a curse. This house, for instance, no harm will come to it. On the other hand, the big mansion on Fifth Avenue, there's a house that needs a lightning rod if ever there was one. I can sense it in my bones."

"He means Mrs. Cavendish's house," Sam explained. "She's the town matron, whatever that is."

Since Collins again had his head down and seemed to have no more to say, I helped myself to another piece of chicken and addressed Felicity. "Do you have any other guests staying at the boardinghouse?"

"Only Fred Dobbs. But he's more of a permanent resident. He's been staying here for several years. He performs odd jobs around town."

"Odd is the right word to describe him if you ask me," interjected Mr. Costello.

Felicity said, "He's a very nice man, even if he has some strange habits. He used to be a professional boxer and suffered some concussions that affected his thinking."

"Where is Dobbs today?" I asked.

"I saw him heading for Indian Charlie's ranch this morning," said Sam. "He'll spend the day out there helping Indian Charlie."

I didn't know what Felicity was referring to when she mentioned Dobb's strange habits, but he'd have to be talented to defeat Silas Collins in a strange contest.

CHAPTER 5

A CONVERSATION WITH FELICITY

A fter lunch, Collins went back to his room for a nap and Costello excused himself to take a walk around town. I thought of following him but preferred to stay and spend a little time with Felicity. I decided to put my pint-sized assistant to use.

I pulled Sam out to the hall, outside hearing range, and asked her if she'd like to do some legwork.

"Sure, but I have to get back to the store before long. I guess I can spare a little time, though."

"Good girl," I said. "I want you to follow Mr. Costello for a while and see where he's going. He won't do anything suspicious during the daytime, but it might help to know his movements."

"Okay," said Sam. "I can tail him like Sam Spade, so he'll never know he's being followed. I'll report back later tonight."

I left Sam to her task and went to the kitchen. It didn't take much convincing for Felicity to let me help with the dishes. "How long will it take to fix your car?" Felicity asked as I dried a plate.

"Hector Suarez says it may take several days. I hope you have a vacancy."

"I always have rooms available. Cordoba isn't a big tourist attraction. I'll show you the room when we finish here."

The room was up the stairs to the left and toward the front of the house, just past Costello's room. This was convenient since for now, he was my main suspect. The room itself was a no-frills affair with just a bed, a dresser, a chair, and a side table, but the room was clean, the bed and chair looked comfortable, and there was plenty of light coming from the window that faced the front of the house. As we headed back down the passageway, Felicity explained the layout.

"The bathroom and shower are on the right just past the stairs. Mr. Costello has the room next to yours. Fred is across from you on the other side of the stairs. Mr. Collins is next to him, across from Mr. Costello. The rest of the rooms are vacant."

She then offered me a cup of coffee and showed me into the parlor. While she went to make the coffee, I inspected the room. All the walls were covered with bookcases, filled with books. There was a fireplace on the back wall and the usual collection of parlor furniture—a well-worn sofa and some worn easy chairs with accompanying coffee table and side tables.

Felicity returned with a tray, upon which were a coffeepot, two cups, and containers of cream and sugar. She placed it on the appropriately named coffee table and we both sat on the sofa.

"You must be quite a reader, judging by your library," I began.

"I like to read," she replied, "but this is the town library, and I am the unofficial town librarian. Anyone can come and borrow a book and return it when they are finished."

"Don't you keep track of who has what?"

"No, we trust each other around here. We have quite a few borrowers, and as you can see, there aren't a lot of books missing. But tell me, what are your first impressions of Cordoba?"

"It seems a nice enough place and the people are friendly, but it seems like it might be a little slow-moving for my taste."

"It might be a dull place for a 'city slicker' like you, but we like it that way. Everybody knows everybody and *likes* everyone. We don't have a lot of modern conveniences, but we do just fine without them."

"What do you do for entertainment? I didn't see a theater or any nightclubs driving in."

"There's a movie theater in Bell City if anyone is interested. But when we want to watch a movie, we watch it here. As well as the town library, this is also the town movie theater. There's a projector and screen out in the hall closet. We set up the screen on the wall opposite the fireplace, move some furniture, add some chairs, and *voila*, instant Grauman's. We're showing *The Big Sleep* tomorrow night if you care to join us. This will be a big hit with Fred, who is a Humphrey Bogart fan, and with your miniature private eye, Sam."

"I'll mark it on my calendar," I said.

Ignoring the sarcastic tone, Felicity continued. "The Cordoba Tavern is the big nightspot. You'll want to stop by tonight to meet some of the locals. I'm sure Ben will be there. There's as much soda drinking as beer. It's just a chance to get together and mingle."

"Yes, what's the deal with that place? Diner by day and bar at night. And Hilda Bluff and Frank Blaine. They live together and each owns half of the place. What's their relationship?"

"Hilda and Frank moved here from back east years ago and brought the diner with them. They bought the house behind the diner, which includes the land where the diner sits. I gather you met Hilda already. You may have a better idea of their relationship once you meet Frank," she said.

I made a note to hit the Cordoba Tavern when it opened and decided to check out the rest of the town. I asked Felicity to be my guide, but she declined, saying she had work to do, and I might find a small-town girl boring anyway. She was wrong about that. I thought she was the prettiest librarian I'd ever seen.

CHAPTER 6

THE FLAGG SISTERS

H aving nothing better to do, I took a stroll around Cordoba and get the lay of the land. This didn't take long. I discovered the town is laid out in a grid consisting of ten streets, five each traveling north to south and east to west. As I have already mentioned, the streets which cross Main Street are First Street through Fifth Avenue. Starting from the west, the streets parallel to Main Street are named Pine Street and Maple Street on one side and Elm Street and Sycamore Street on the other. This is unusual since none of the trees named (nor any other trees) grow in Cordoba. These streets might be more accurately named Yucca Street, Yucca Street, Yucca Street, and Tumbleweed Lane. The only truthfully named street is Main Street since it is indeed the most traveled street in Cordoba.

After surveying the town, my first stop was the general store to see if Sam had anything to report. She was behind the counter munching another bag of Planters. In between bites, she reported that Costello had wandered around town for about half an hour before walking down Elm Street to talk to the Flagg sisters.

"They own the house across the street from Hilda and Frank," Sam informed me. "He talked to the sisters for about five minutes and then went in the diner, and he's been there ever since. I've been keeping an eye on the diner from over here, and he hasn't left yet."

I complimented Sam on her investigative skills and asked her if the Flagg sisters would still be home at this time of day. She assured me they seldom went out and spent each day sitting on their front porch chatting with passersby. I decided to pass by and have a talk with the sisters myself and maybe case out the Bluff-Blaine residence while I was at it.

Several minutes later I was walking down Elm Street and came across three elderly women sitting on a swing on the front porch. The swing was wide enough for all three but a little high off the ground, so the ladies had to reach on tiptoes to swing back and forth, which they were doing without speaking. As I approached, the first thing I noticed was that the Flagg sisters, for that was them, were appropriately named. The three ladies, in their eighties at least, were seated side by side as I mentioned, and from left to right, the color of each sister's hair was red, white, and blue. The first sister's hair was dyed bright red, the second a natural white, and the third was a wispy light blue like you see on some elderly women.

The ladies, seeing me coming, tilted their heads and leaned forward in unison like birds on a telephone wire. As I moved closer the heads turned, again in unison, to stay focused on my movements.

"Hello, ladies, how are we doing today?" I shouted as I grew nearer.

"We're doing fine," said the first, followed by "fine" from the second and another "fine" from the third. I soon learned that every sentence from one of the sisters, who were named Ruth (red), Mabel (white), and Jewell (blue), was either repeated or finished by one or both of the others.

"This is quite a momentous day," Mabel said—it was her turn to speak first—followed by Jewell saying, "because you're the second stranger we've met today and," back to Ruth, "we normally don't have any strangers around here at all."

I introduced myself and explained why I was in town and inquired about the first stranger.

"Just a little while ago, there was a large Italian man named Abbott."

"No, it was Bracomonte."

"I think it was Turley."

Back to Mabel. "He was very nice and seemed very interested in the people across the street."

"But we couldn't tell him very much." (Jewell)

Back to Ruth, "Because we seldom see them. Occasionally, late at night or early in the morning, we hear them talking."

"Or arguing," Mabel interjected.

"Not that we're snooping," finished Jewell.

I looked across the street. Frank and Hilda's house was located across the street from the Flagg house. The landscape sloped up from Elm Street to the center of town, so Frank and Hilda's house stood above the Flagg house and the diner was higher still. I noticed that the sisters had an unobstructed view of both.

I was then offered a glass of lemonade, which they kept on a table on the porch for people who passed by, I think as an inducement for them to stay a while longer. Since I had nowhere else to be for a while and the temperature was at least ninety-five degrees in the shade (if there was any shade in this town), I accepted the offer.

For the next half hour, I sat on the porch steps and drank lemonade while the Flagg sisters rocked and told tales of their lives. None of the three had ever married. Ruth was the adventurous one and had traveled around the country in her younger days. She spoke fondly of an affair with a riverboat captain on the Mississippi and of drinking absinthe in the French Quarter with shady characters, both black and white, who had duels in the bayou and sometimes fought each other with Bowie knives while she sipped her absinthe. The other two sisters dismissed these stories as pure balderdash.

Mabel had found religion and had been attending the church down the street three times a week since childhood. The church, as best as I could make out, was a nondenominational church that had been around since the town was founded in the 1850s and was named the "Friendly Church for the Salvation of All Souls, Including Gunslingers and Indians."

Jewell had a full-time job keeping Ruth and Mabel on the right track and making sure the lemonade was made every noontime.

As I wrapped up my visit, I inquired about the intruder they had seen behind the diner. All three sisters agreed they had only seen the prowler once but did not get a good look at the face. They also couldn't be sure if it was a man or a woman.

"We can't see so good anymore at our age."

"Not that we would snoop."

"But we haven't seen any strangers around except you and that nice Mr. Benedetto."

"O'Boyle!"

"Turley!"

Then three voices in unison, "Come by tomorrow for some lemonade."

I told them I would try to return tomorrow if sufficiently recovered from today's visit and went on my way.

As I left, I thought the poor vision the three ladies possessed may have been enhanced by the telescope I had seen in the front attic window of their house. The telescope seemed to be pointing in the direction of the diner.

CHAPTER 7

THE REST OF THE AFTERNOON

After my head had cleared, I wandered over to the gas station to see Hector and determine if there was any progress on the car. Hector confirmed that my car had been towed to Bell City. Other than that, he had no updates. I asked where I might find Ben Nye, and Hector suggested I try the municipal building, which was just down the block.

"That's where the mayor's office is," Hector informed me, "but he might be there anyway."

The municipal building was a small square brick building with a sign out front informing me that in addition to the mayor's office, the building also housed the sheriff's office, jail, tax collector, and sanitary commission.

I walked in and headed down the corridor to the mayor's office, which a sign told me was in the back of the building on the left. On the way I passed the sheriff's office and jail on the front left, both of which appeared to be empty, as did the tax collector and sanitary commission offices on the right.

No one was in Ben's office either. I waited a few minutes, but when Ben didn't return, I decided to try to catch him at the diner. As I was passing the sheriff's office, I heard faint sounds coming from inside. Entering the office, I found it empty and proceeded to the cell in the rear. The cell door was open and the cot in the cell was occupied by Ben Nye, snoring. I shook him to wake him up. After he got his bearings, he brought me back to his office, showed me to a seat opposite his desk, and offered me a cup of coffee from a pot on a table in a corner of the office. I turned down his offer and asked how he liked being mayor of a bustling town like Cordoba.

He laughed and said, "It's not much of a town, but then I'm not much of a mayor either. The mayor of Cordoba has few duties other than riding in the first car of the St. Patrick's Day parade. This is a small honor seeing as it's the only car in the parade.

"But I can't complain," he continued. "I get by okay. I don't get paid much, but there's nothing to spend money on around here anyway. And I get to take plenty of naps," he said, motioning toward the sheriff's office.

"Life around here is slow," Ben continued, "and we may be twenty or thirty years behind the times, but the people are friendly and the beer is even cold over at the tavern. You should consider settling out here and get away from the rat race. You might live a lot longer out here without the pollution and temptations of the city."

"No thanks," I replied. "I wouldn't live any longer—it would just seem longer. No offense, but I plan on escaping this time capsule as soon as my car is fixed."

"Suit yourself," Ben said. "What's the latest on the car?"

I told him the car had been towed and that it would take a few days to fix.

"Which reminds me," I said, "I better pick up a few items since I planned this as a day trip. Is there a store in town where I can buy some things?"

"Nothing in Cordoba, unless you want to pick up a pair of overalls and some socks down at the general store. There's a department store in Bell City where you can get what you need. You can borrow my car. It's parked right out front and the keys are in the ignition. You can check on the progress of your car while you're there."

I took Ben up on his offer and headed out of town in the opposite direction from which I arrived. The trip took about twenty minutes, and I would describe the scenery on the way but there wasn't any.

Bell City was what San Diegan's would consider a backwater town and what the citizens of Cordoba call the big city. It had a movie theater that surprisingly wasn't showing a 1940s gangster movie, a few restaurants, and a small department store, where I purchased enough clothing and toiletries to hold me over for a few days. I had passed Harry's Service Center on the way in, so I backtracked and checked in with Harry. He confirmed through closed lips that had a cigarette dangling from one side that my axle would need replacing and that it would take at least three days and maybe a week to get the parts and do the job.

With that depressing news, I headed back to Cordoba. I returned Ben's car and walked to the boardinghouse to freshen up. I found Felicity in the parlor reading. Something that smelled good cooked in the kitchen. There was no one else around, so I went up to my room, dropped off my purchases, and headed off to the shower. This turned out to be a bath since the bathroom did not include a shower. I soaked in the tub awhile, got dressed, and went downstairs for supper, which was just about ready. By this time Felicity was busy in the kitchen. There was no sign of Silas Collins or Dobbs, but Costello was in the parlor reading a magazine. I took one of the easy chairs and asked him how his day went.

"Not bad," he said. "I stopped by and talked to the old sisters who live behind the diner—they insisted I come back tomorrow for more lemonade—and then went to the diner for some dessert after Felicity's excellent lunch. I talked awhile with the girl Samantha at the general store. I seem to see her all over town," he said with a smile.

Before he could continue, Felicity came in and informed us that supper was served.

Tonight's menu included pot roast, mashed potatoes and gravy, succotash, and homemade biscuits. A man Felicity introduced as Fred Dobbs came in and joined us a few minutes after we started and apologized for being late. He had been working at Indian Charlie's ranch and lost track of time. He was a tall, well-built black man of about sixty or seventy with a full head of graying hair and a crooked nose and swollen ears that gave away his former profession.

I inquired about the work he did at the ranch.

"Indian Charlie has a ranch a mile out of town where he grows miniature cactus, you know, the kind that are several inches high, the kind they sell in flower stores," Dobbs said. "He has a few acres of cactus growing that I help pick. It's not hard work except on your feet unless you're careful. Indian Charlie, he doesn't mind. He walks around barefoot, and he'll step on one of those little cactuses and just pull the spines out of his feet, but me, I wear work shoes and those little needles still get through to my feet so I can hardly walk."

The rest of the supper transpired with little conversation as everyone was busy eating. When dinner was finished, Dobbs excused himself to go upstairs and clean up and soak his feet, Costello returned to his magazine in the parlor, and Felicity and I headed to the kitchen to do the dishes. This time I washed, and she dried.

"I'm thinking about heading over to the tavern in a little while to soak up some of the local color and a few beers, if you'd care to join me," I offered.

"Thanks for the invitation, but I promised Sam I would be over later to play games with the family. You're welcome to join us if you like."

I begged off—as much as I enjoy a rousing game of Monopoly— since I wanted to check out the tavern and the local folks.

CHAPTER 8

THE CORDOBA TAVERN

T he weather had cooled in the early evening as I strolled down Main Street toward the diner that was now a tavern. There were few people on the street, but I met Phil Childers, who had just locked up the store and was crossing the street to enter the tavern.

"Good evening, Phil," I said when we met on the sidewalk out front. "I was surprised to see you locking the door to the store. Nobody seems to lock anything around here."

"Not much crime to speak of," Phil said. "I lock it more to keep it from blowing open if the wind picks up. The door jamb is a little warped."

As we entered the tavern, I noticed the diner sign had been removed from the door. Instead, there was a knotty pine signpost stuck in the dirt to the left of the entrance with the words "Cordoba Tavern" burned into the wood. Inside, everything looked the same but different. Same counter, same seats, same booths, but the atmosphere seemed to have changed. On the counter bowls of peanuts and pretzels had replaced bowls of fruit. A few bottles of low-end liquor had replaced the boxes of cereal on the shelves behind the counter. A couple of taps were installed in the middle of the counter. The tap handles did not have names, so I couldn't tell what kind of beer it was, but judging from my overall impression of the town, I assumed the two taps represented leaded and unleaded.

Ben was seated at the same spot as earlier in the day, close to the jukebox. To his left was an elderly gentleman, at least seventy. At the other end of the bar, Silas Collins was drinking a beer and talking to an old-timer dressed in dusty old clothes and wearing

Jed Clampett's hat. There were two somewhat younger couples occupying a booth in the front of the tavern. The only other person in the bar was the bartender, who I assumed was Frank Blaine. He was clean-shaven with a weathered face and was as thin as Hilda Bluff was stout. I still hadn't discovered what their relationship was, but Frank was the Jack Spratt of the pair.

Frank's cadaverous facial features sort of resembled Hilda's if you added a few pounds of flesh around them, so I thought it was more likely that they were brother and sister than husband and wife. Of course, I thought they could be unrelated. My wonderings were interrupted when Ben motioned for us to join him.

Phil and I took the two seats to the right of Ben, with me in the middle. After we were seated Ben introduced me to the man on his left.

"This is Doc Fletcher, the best doctor in town."

"Pleased to meet you," Doc said. "As you can guess, I'm the *only* doctor in town, and I don't get a great deal of business. How do you like our town?"

"Don't ask him that, Doc," Ben jumped in before I could answer. "He'll be ready to leave as soon as his car is fixed."

I corrected him. "I was going to say, 'A little slow for my taste, but I like the people.'"

"Met anybody interesting since you been in town?" asked Phil.

"Well, I met the Flagg sisters this morning."

"How was the lemonade?" asked Phil. "You know, they make it fresh-squeezed every day. Throw away what isn't drunk by the end of the day, so they don't disappoint their next day's guests."

"The lemonade was very good…"

Doc interrupted. "They've lived here all their lives. I've been treating them since we were all young."

"I got the impression that Ruth had traveled a bit," I said.

"Oh, she has, she has," Doc replied, "but only in her mind. She's never been further than Bell City, but her imagination has taken her to many strange and exotic locations. Still, can you think of a better way to travel? It's cheap, you don't need a passport, and you don't have to pack."

"I guess you have a point there," I said. Perry Como sang "Catch a Falling Star" on the jukebox. "The only other people I've met are little Samantha and Felicity and the roomers at the boardinghouse."

Ben smiled and winked at me. "That Felicity would be a real catch for any man. She's pretty and cooks great and has a nice little business in the boardinghouse. Plus, there's not much competition in these parts."

"I guess you're right, if a man wanted to settle down, but that's not me," I said, trying to convince myself as well as Ben since I had been having the same thoughts.

"Me, I'm a confirmed bachelor," said Ben, "but take Phil here; he's been married to his Phyllis for years and never had a fight."

"Best ten years of my life," said Phil.

"Oh, you've been married ten years?" I asked.

"No, I've been married for thirty, but ten of them have been great," Phil joked.

"Don't let Phyllis hear you say that," cautioned Doc. "She might not find it funny."

"She says the same about me," Phil said, "except she reduces it to three good years." He grabbed a handful of pretzels and continued, "Phyllis is over at Bert and Millie's house—that's Sam's parents and Felicity's brother and sister-in-law—for game night."

"I got an invitation, but came here instead," I said.

"Well, glad you made it over," Phil said, and then, in mock anger, "Can't a couple of thirsty men get a beer around here?"

Frank, who was down the end of the bar talking to Silas, said, "Hold your horses, Phil. I'll be down in a minute."

Frank Sinatra sang "Love Is a Many-Splendored Thing."

By the time Frank made his way to our end of the bar, we were listening to Nat King Cole's version of "Stardust." After I was introduced to Frank, I made the mistake of asking what kind of beer he was serving.

"We've got two kinds," he said. "We've got Fromova beer and we've got Somotha beer."

"I've never heard of them—are they local brands?" I asked.

"Yeah," replied Frank in a raspy voice. "One's brewed by a fella fromova in Bell City, and the other is brewed by somotha guy in another town around here."

Bing Crosby sang "Moonlight Serenade."

I ordered the Fromova, which was served in a diner glass. Surprisingly, it was cold and drinkable. As I drank, I asked Ben about the old gent talking to Silas.

"That's Lucky O'Leary," Ben explained. "He's a miner who's been around here for about a year. He lives out in the desert and he's searching for the Lost Dutchman's mine."

"The Lost Dutchman's mine?" I was confused. "Isn't that supposed to be in southern Arizona?"

"Yes," Ben replied, "but he's using a map he bought at a souvenir shop in Arizona, and the copy he got was a misprint. The lettering was added upside down, so Lucky has been reading the map upside down. He determined that the X on the map was the starting point, and he ended up in Cordoba."

"Judging by his appearance, he doesn't seem to be too lucky," I countered.

Phil said, "He's called Lucky the way a big man is nicknamed Tiny and a bald man is called Curly."

This seemed like enough of an explanation to Ben, so he changed the subject and asked how I liked things over at the boardinghouse. I told him I liked the accommodations and the food, as he mentioned, was outstanding.

"What do you think of your fellow boarders?" Doc asked.

"I'm not sure. Costello seems a little secretive, and Collins has some interesting views on lightning. Dobbs seems like a nice guy."

"Fred C. Dobbs. He's a strange one," Phil said. "His father was a big Humphrey Bogart fan and named Fred after Bogart's character in *Treasure of the Sierra Madre*. Fred C. Dobbs. The C doesn't stand for anything."

Ben picked up the story. "He was a boxer in his earlier years, known as Kid Caramel. He had a lot of fights and won a few but never made it to the big bouts. His punch didn't pack much of a wallop. He was great at blocking punches. Unfortunately, he blocked most of them with either his face or his midsection."

It was Doc's turn. I was beginning to feel like I was talking to the Flagg sisters again. "Still, he was a well-built, good-looking fighter. One writer described him as Sugar Ray Robinson without the talent. His last fight was a fifteen-rounder with a middleweight contender. The Kid was knocked down eleven times and got back up ten. He never entered the ring again."

Phil continued. "He came out pretty well, except he now has stretches, when he's been drinking, where he thinks he's a character from a Humphrey Bogart movie. It started with Fred C. Dobbs, but now he's developed a whole repertoire of Bogart characters.

"Some nights he's Duke Mantee or Charlie Allnut or Rick from *Casablanca* or Captain Queeg, playing with ball bearings and complaining about missing strawberries. He might be Sam Spade or Philip Marlowe, but those two are hard to distinguish one from another. If he comes in tonight, you may get a demonstration."

As if on cue, Dobbs walked in and took a seat in a booth near the jukebox. He said hello to everyone as he passed. Frank drew a beer and brought it over to him with a bowl of pretzels. He was on his second beer and hadn't said a word since he sat down when a stunning blonde wearing a short, tight skirt and equally tight blouse and high heels walked in. She headed toward us. The other patrons greeted her with "Hi, Leo," as she walked by, except for Dobbs, who muttered, "Of all the gin joints in all the towns in all the world, she walks into mine." Suddenly the Kid was in Casablanca and the tavern was Rick's Café Americain.

Without losing a step, Leo headed over to the Kid's booth and sat down opposite him.

"Hello, Rick," she said, keeping him in character. "It's been a long time. Paris, I think it was."

"I remember every detail," Rick said. "The Germans wore gray and you wore blue."

"It's good to see you again," Leo said as she got up and walked over to us.

Ben introduced her as Doc's receptionist.

"You're the prettiest Leo I ever met," I flirted.

She smiled and said, "My name's Leonora, but I wasn't fond of being called Nora, so Leo it is."

She then walked over to Doc and gave him a kiss that showed she was a great deal more than just his receptionist.

"Let's get a booth where we can be alone," she said to Doc, and to me as she was leaving, "Nice to meet you, Milo."

Doc stopped as he passed me and leaned in. "If you get a chance tomorrow, drop into my office. I have a little mystery myself that might be right up your alley."

Another lost dog, I suspected. I told Doc I would try to squeeze him in between my visit to the Flagg sisters and a long side trip to Boredom. Doc chuckled and walked away with Leo. Looking at the two, I said, "Doc's a lucky guy."

"Sure is," said Ben. "Leo is a heck of a receptionist."

"That's not what I was thinking about," I said.

"I know," replied Ben. "By the way, in addition to being his receptionist, Leo is also Doc's wife?"

Echoing my thoughts, Dean Martin sang, "Ain't That a Kick in the Head" on the jukebox.

"That's not what I want to hear," piped the Kid from his booth. His words seemed to be directed at me. "You know what I want to hear, Sam. Play it."

Thinking back to the movie, I said, "I don't think I remember it, boss."

"You played it for her, you can play it for me."

Phil leaned in and whispered, "Drop a dime in the jukebox. E-7. There's change in the tray on the sill next to the jukebox."

I did as instructed. Soon the room filled with the sounds of Dooley Wilson singing "As Time Goes By." Frank brought the Kid another beer and he sat silently listening to the music.

It was now getting late in the Cordoba time zone, about 9 p.m., and the bar was emptying out. Doc and Leo got up from their booth. Before leaving, Leo walked over to the Kid's table and said to him, "We'll always have Paris."

The Kid replied, "That's my line."

"I know," replied Leo. She then leaned in and kissed him on the cheek and walked back to the door. As the Kid watched her leave, a single tear ran down his cheek. As I watched Leo leave, I saw a matching tear on her face.

"That's enough for me, also," said Ben, lightening up the mood. "If I stay up too late, I'll sleep right through my nap tomorrow."

Phil also got up to leave, so I joined them. I said my good-byes and walked over to Fred's booth. "C'mon, Kid. It's time to go home."

He got up, dropped a dollar on the table, and we walked out together.

Not much was said on the way back to the boardinghouse. After we climbed up the stairs, the Kid headed to his room and I
headed to mine. As we both were about to enter our rooms, the
Kid hollered across the railing.

"Louie, I think this is the beginning of a beautiful friendship."

CHAPTER 9

A VISIT TO THE DOCTOR

The next day I awoke earlier than usual. I was a late sleeper in San Diego, but here I was awake and alert at seven. Maybe it was the fresh desert air coming in through the window or maybe it was the smell of bacon and eggs and fresh coffee wafting up the stairway, but I was up, dressed, and downstairs sitting at the dining room table in ten minutes.

Costello and Silas Collins were also waiting for Felicity, and she didn't keep us waiting, entering with a big platter of bacon and eggs in one hand and a pot of coffee in the other.

"Good morning, gentlemen," she said. "Breakfast is served. You can have your eggs any way you like them, as long as you like them scrambled. If you want them any other way, you can take a walk down to the diner. Dig in and I'll be right back with the toast."

After a little small talk and a lot of breakfast, everyone arose from the table.

"I reckon I'll head out and see if I can sell a few lightning rods," said Silas as he turned toward the front door.

"I shall also take the opportunity this fine day provides to take a stroll," Costello said. "I'll see you later."

I was in no hurry, so I again helped Felicity with the cleanup.

"We're getting to be like an old married couple, doing the dishes together like this," Felicity said. "We better be careful, or people will start talking."

I laughed and replied, "From my observations, once people are married, that's when they stop doing the dishes together and find separate activities to get away from each other."

"That's a pretty cynical view of marriage right there," Felicity came back. "Are you speaking from experience?"

"No, just from using my keen observational skills when I'm around married couples."

The dishes were finished, so we headed to the parlor to have coffee and continue the conversation.

"I don't know who you base your theory on, but most of the married couples around here are very happy together," Felicity said. "Sure, they have their arguments and differences, but they enjoy being around each other. My brother Bert and his wife Millie have been married for ten years and have two lovely children, and they still act like newlyweds."

"Speaking of Bert and Millie, how was game night?" I asked, changing the subject, since I think I had hit a nerve. "Did you go for a game of Monopoly or just break out the old Ouija board?"

Felicity frowned. "Go ahead and be sarcastic if you like, but everyone enjoyed it. And we ended up playing Clue since Sam insists on showing off her detective skills since you arrived in town. She won most of the games, with Phyllis Childers coming in second."

"That's Phil's wife, isn't it? I was down at the tavern with Phil last night." I was tempted to remark about married couples having separate activities, but decided not to venture again into those waters, which seemed to be shark-infested. "By the way, Doc Fletcher and his wife seem to be quite a couple."

"There is an age difference and they look mismatched, but Doc and Leo are one of those happily married couples I was referring to earlier. She acts a little older than her age and he acts younger than his, so they sort of meet in the middle."

"How did they meet?"

"She's been his patient since she was a little girl, then she became his receptionist when she got older. After Doc's first wife died of cancer several years ago, the relationship blossomed into romance."

"Speaking of Doc Fletcher, I told him I would drop by to see him today. It seems he has something he wants my professional opinion on."

"I can't think of why Doc would need the services of a detective"—she said the word *detective* as if her mouth were full of dirt— "but if you need directions, he's on Third Street, the next street over. Turn right as you go out the door, make another right at the corner, then make a left onto Third Street and his office is about halfway down the block."

I figured now was as good a time as any, so I got up to leave. I wasn't sure what I would do for the rest of the day until a remark from Felicity reminded me I had plans.

"The Tri-County Fair is in full swing if you need something to do," she said.

"That's right, Ben invited me to join him. Will you be going?" I asked as I headed for the door.

"I may go later with Bert and Millie and the kids. Maybe I'll see you there."

The afternoon heat had not arrived yet and the temperature was comfortable for a morning walk. As I strolled down the sidewalk, I heard footsteps running behind me. I turned around to see Sam gaining on me.

When she approached, she slowed down and said, out of breath, "I was afraid I'd missed you. Mom insisted that I eat all my breakfast and help with the dishes before I left the house."

"You needn't have worried," I replied. "Your Aunt Felicity insisted that I do the same."

"What are we doing today?" Sam asked.

"I am headed over to Doc Fletcher's office, but don't you have anywhere you have to be?"

"Nope. School's out and I don't have to be at the store until noon."

"Well, you're welcome to tag along."

As we walked Sam asked if Mr. Costello had said anything about her following him yesterday. I lied and told her Costello hadn't mentioned it.

"I guess I shadowed him pretty good then," she said proudly.

"I guess you did," I lied again.

Doc's office turned out to be in his house, a pleasant-looking older building guarded by shade trees out front. His waiting room was to the right, off the hall. The waiting room was empty when we entered except for Leo, who was behind the desk at the far end of the room rifling through some papers. Other than Leo, there was nothing remarkable in the room. There were about a dozen straight-backed chairs for patients, and the walls of the room were covered by medical charts and several Norman Rockwell prints in plastic frames. The tables were stacked with the usual supply of magazines.

Leo looked up as we entered. "Hi, Sam. And Milo. Nice to see you again. Did you get Fred home yesterday? We saw you leaving after we left."

"Yes, we managed to find the boardinghouse with little trouble."

"That was nice of you to take Fred home. Sometimes I worry about him, but he always seems to find his way. But what brings you here? I hope you're feeling all right."

"He's fine," Sam chimed in. "We're here to see Doc about some detective work."

"I can't imagine why Doc would need detective work," Leo smiled, "but have a seat and Doc will see you. He's with a patient right now."

We sat down and I picked up a magazine from the table to kill time. I discovered that the *Reader's Digest* I'd picked up was dated 1957, even older than most I've seen in doctors' offices. After reading an ad and deciding I wasn't interested in purchasing a Kelvinator, I searched for a more current magazine among the pile, but all the other magazines—with various titles, some now extinct—were of the same vintage.

We were only seated for a few minutes when the door behind Leo's desk opened and Doc walked out with Silas Collins. Silas had a bandage wrapped around one of his fingers.

Doc saw us and came over, touching Leo affectionately on the shoulder on the way past. Silas stopped at the desk to talk to Leo.

"Thanks for stopping by," the doctor said. "Come into my office and we can discuss my problem."

"Can I come too, Doc?" asked Sam. "I'm Milo's assistant."

Doc laughed and said, "I guess so, so long as you're Milo's assistant, but promise to keep what you hear confidential. I wouldn't want it to get out all over town."

"Cross my heart and hope to die," Sam said, giving the appropriate cross as we headed for Doc's office.

We entered through the door behind Leo's desk into a narrow hallway that ran to the back of the building, with three doorways on the left. The first room was the examination room, which I could view through the open door. The second door, also open, led to a small supply closet. Doc's office was the last room on the left. It was furnished with a plain-looking desk and chair, a couple of visitor's chairs matching the chairs in the waiting room on the opposite side of the desk from Doc's chair, and a well-worn sofa against the wall on the left. Next to the sofa was an end table stacked high with more old magazines.

Doc motioned us to the visitor's seats and sat in his swivel chair and leaned back. After a little small talk, he said, "I guess you could tell by the looks of the waiting room and my office that I have accumulated quite a collection of magazines."

"I did notice there were quite a few copies of older issues," I said.

"Well," he said, "I've been collecting magazines ever since I opened my office many years ago, first as reading material for my patients, and then I got into more serious collecting. Nothing current but copies of old magazines from the forties through the sixties—*Life, Look, The Saturday Evening Post, Reader's Digest, TV Guide*, magazines like that, some of which went out of business a long time ago. I've obtained complete copies of several issues over the years, but instead of keeping them locked up where they are of no use, I leave them in the waiting room for the patients to read. I have a whole collection in the supply room next door, and I rotate the copies I put out in the waiting room.

"Well, sir," he continued, "I straighten out the issues at the end of the day. Last Tuesday when I was stacking the magazines in the waiting room, I noticed that two of the issues were missing. I always place ten copies out so I can keep track and change them every month. On Monday there were ten issues. On Tuesday there were only eight."

"Were you able to identify the specific issues that were missing?" I asked Doc.

He nodded. "One was the issue of *Look* and the other was a *TV Guide*, both with December 1954 dates. I put magazines of the same time period out."

"Do you know if there is any connection between the two issues?"

"Not that I know of. I have not read every issue in my collection. Occasionally, I pick one up at random and peruse it, but it's mostly the fun of collecting. It's not a big deal if I'm missing a few issues, but I'm curious to know what happened to them."

"I'll see what I can dig up," I said. "Can you give me a list of the patients you saw that day?"

"Leo can check the appointment book and tell you. I'll be glad to pay you your usual fee."

"No charge, Doc. I'm doing work for Ben anyway, so I'll be keeping my eyes open around town. Besides, in my line of business, a man might need a doctor at some point, especially in a dangerous town like Cordoba."

Doc laughed as Sam and I went out to the reception desk. I asked Leo for a list of the patients Doc had seen last Tuesday.

"Let's see," she said as she checked her appointment book. "Indian Charlie was in to have cactus spines removed from his feet. This is pretty much a regular occurrence for him. Mrs. Cavendish was in early in the afternoon. There was nothing wrong with her, but she's a confirmed hypochondriac. And the only other patient was that Mr. Costello. He was complaining of stomach pains, which turned out to be indigestion."

So much for patient confidentiality, I thought as I reached for a piece of paper to write all this down, but I noticed that Sam was taking notes in a small notebook with a brown cover, spiral bound at the top. Relieved of my note-taking duties, I said to Leo, "You know, they have computers these days that can keep track of all that information."

"We don't need them. Besides, it's hard to get any kind of service out here in the middle of nowhere. That's why you won't see any cell phones in town. You know that telephone company commercial that says they cover ninety-seven percent of the country? Well, we're in the other three percent. Also, we're limited to a few TV channels we can pick up with antennas from the broadcast tower near the highway. No cable companies operate out here. Someone could get a satellite dish if they could find someone to come out and install it, but nobody bothers. We don't miss what we don't have."

"I have to admit that it was kind of pleasant sitting at the tavern last night without seeing a line of smartphones sitting on the bar," I said. "Did you notice any of the patients acting unusual?"

"No. I'm sure both Mrs. Cavendish and Mr. Costello were looking at magazines, but I'm not sure about Indian Charlie."

"Thanks," I said and started to leave, but Leo called me back. Sam said she would wait on the porch. I returned to the reception desk.

Leo said in a concerned voice, "I know this seems like a trivial matter and Doc does not seem to be taking it seriously, but he prizes his magazine collection, and this hurt him a great deal, not only the fact that the magazines were missing but that someone would take them. I hope you take the investigation seriously."

"I will," I said. "You worry about Doc a great deal, don't you?"

"I love him very much. If you're referring to the difference in our ages, I can assure you that Lucky O'Leary is the only gold digger in town."

"I wasn't..."

Leo cut me off. "It's okay." She laughed. "I get the look all the time from strangers. I've been Doc's patient since I was a little girl. As I grew up, I realized that he was the kindest, gentlest grown-up in town. Also, he was quite handsome when he was younger, with sandy hair and bright, beautiful gray eyes, and I had a huge crush on him as a teenager. Well, I guess the crush never went away, even after I started working as his receptionist. When his first wife died of cancer several years ago, we became closer. We've been married now for three years, and sometimes at night when we're sitting in the living room reading, me with a romance novel and Doc with one of his magazines, I'll look at him and if I look deep into his eyes, I still see the gentle, jolly, sandy-haired doctor with the sparkling eyes."

"Well, don't worry," I said, "I'll get to the bottom of this for Doc and you."

CHAPTER 10

A VISIT WITH MRS. CAVENDISH

I walked out of Doc's house and onto the porch, where I found Sam sitting on the top step of the porch reading her notes with a serious expression on her face, munching on the ever-present bag of peanuts.

"What's our next step," I asked, sitting down next to her.

"Well," she said, "I think we should concentrate on the people who had access to the magazines last Tuesday. I think we can eliminate Doc and Leo."

"I agree," I said seriously.

"That leaves Indian Charlie, Mrs. Cavendish, and Mr. Costello. Indian Charlie wouldn't take the magazines to read, but he might want to fence them."

"That wouldn't be too easy to do in these parts," I responded.

"You're right. Mrs. Cavendish doesn't need the money. She can be bossy and cranky, but I think she's a pretty good person underneath. Besides, both Indian Charlie and Mrs. Cavendish live in Cordoba and know how much the magazines mean to Doc, so I don't think they would take them."

"That leaves Mr. Costello."

"That's what I was thinking. He's a stranger in town and may also be involved in the snooping down at the diner. Maybe the two cases are connected."

"Maybe, but what would be his motive for stealing old magazines? What motive would the other two have?"

"I guess that's what we have to find out."

"I'm thinking the two magazines that were taken were not random choices. Both the *Look* and the *TV Guide* were published in December 1954. Maybe there were articles in each that somebody didn't want anyone to see. But that will be difficult to determine since I'm sure there are no copies of either magazine lying around in Cordoba."

"What do we do next?" asked Sam.

"Why don't you run back to the boardinghouse and check for magazines in the parlor. It's a long shot, but I saw Costello reading a magazine in the parlor yesterday."

"Maybe he was reading an article and took the magazine with him to finish it."

"But in that case, he wouldn't take two magazines."

"Maybe two different people took the magazines."

"I think we've got too many *maybes* and not enough *surelys* to solve the case at this point. While you head back to the boardinghouse, I'll pay a visit to Mrs. Cavendish. Can you point me in the right direction?"

"She lives two blocks over on Fifth Avenue. It's a big house and you won't have any trouble finding it," she said as she smiled. Then she took off running back to the boardinghouse.

Even at this point in the morning, the weather was heating up, but the walk was short, so I wasn't much bothered. When I reached the corner of Fifth Avenue and Elm Street, I realized what Sam had meant when she said I couldn't miss the Cavendish residence. The building was about as close as you could get to a mansion in a town like Cordoba, situated on a slight hill and surrounded by a lush green lawn, the first grass I had seen since I came to town. A fellow outside was watering the grass from a garden hose. Around the lawn, several barn swallows were gobbling up worms, no doubt courtesy of the Hector Suarez Gas Station and Bait Shop.

The building and grounds were surrounded by a wrought-iron fence with posts which came to a point at the top. Standing outside the gate and admiring the handiwork was Silas Collins. I approached him and said hello.

"Pretty good workmanship on the fence," he said. "I don't understand why people will install a fence to protect their property, but balk at installing a lightning rod to protect their house."

"Is that why you're here, to sell the old lady a lightning rod?" I asked.

"Yup, just trying to do her a favor. Her manservant, or what-ever he is over there watering the lawn, said I had to wait here because she was eating breakfast. She'll be receiving guests at her normal visiting hour, between ten and eleven."

Since it was a quarter to ten when I arrived, I hung around.

"You said at dinner last night that this house needs a lightning rod. How can you tell?"

"It's not the type of house or a physical feature," said Silas. "I can tell by my senses. The way the wind moves around a house, the smell of the air, whether the hair on my arms stands up when I enter the building. I imagine you've seen lightning often enough, and heard the thunder, but have you smelled it and tasted it and felt the way the air moves around it? It's got a purpose like every-thing else in life and a target, and you must use your senses to tell what the target is. My senses tell me this house is a target."

By this time, it was ten o'clock, and the man who had been wa-tering the lawn approached and shortened our conversation.

"Mrs. Cavendish declines to see you," he said, addressing Silas with an English accent. "She informed you yesterday she was not interested in purchasing a lightning rod." Turning to me he said, "And who are you and what is your business with Mrs. Caven-dish? She doesn't hold much stock with peddlers." He flashed a disapproving glance at Silas.

"I'm not selling anything," I said, as nicely as I could under the circumstances. "I'm just in town visiting the mayor, and he sug-gested I stop by and pay my respects to Mrs. Cavendish," I lied. I was hoping Ben's name would carry weight with the old girl.

It at least got me through the gate. "Come with me," said Jeeves, or whatever his name was, "and I'll announce you to see if Mrs. Cavendish will see you."

Silas turned to leave and muttered, "I was just trying to help her."

"Tough luck," I said to him. Somehow, I got the feeling he was the lucky one being denied access to Mrs. Cavendish.

As he walked away, I thought of our conversation and hollered after him, "And if any mysterious carnivals should arrive in Cor-doba by train in the dead of night in the next few days, I'd advise you to stay as far away as possible."

At this, he turned and said, "Much obliged for the advice, Mr. Forbes," and continued down the street.

I followed Mrs. C's man down the path to the house like a man walking the last mile. When we entered the hall, I was directed to a sitting room on the left of the hall that contained more chairs, and of a much higher quality than those in Doc's waiting room.

"Wait here and I'll see if Mrs. Cavendish will see you," said Lurch. He returned a moment later and said with a look of distaste, "Follow me."

He led me into the room across the hall. It was decorated in Victorian style, with a large chandelier in the middle of the room. The sofa and chairs all had legs with lions standing on balls carved into them, and they were upholstered in a heavy fabric with a Jacobean design. There was a fireplace across from the entrance, and to my amazement, a blazing fire was burning. As I approached, the temperature seemed to rise with each step I took. Above the fireplace, I noticed a painting of a young man and woman, posed next to each other.

Sitting to the left of the fireplace was an old woman in her eighties or nineties whom I assumed was Mrs. Cavendish. It took me a while to focus on her due to the rapid onset of heatstroke and because the pattern on her dress almost exactly matched the pattern of the chair, she was seated in. She blended so perfectly, it gave the impression that there was nothing there except a floating head and two hands on the arms of the chair.

Although on in years, she had an upright posture and a face that still possessed some of the beauty she had had in her younger years. Her hair was snow white and tightly tied in a bun in back, giving her a stern and somber appearance.

"Please come in and take a seat, Mr. Forbes," she said, motioning to the sofa and chairs around her with a wave of a spectral hand.

"Pleased to meet you, Mrs. Cavendish," I responded as I chose a chair as far away from the fire as possible while still being within listening distance.

Noticing my choice of seat, Mrs. C said with a hint of a smile, "I apologize for the fire, but my bones can't handle the cold like they used to. I know it's a little early, but feel free to have a drink.

Doctor Fletcher forbids me to drink anymore, so I get my pleasure watching others indulge."

She motioned to a silver tray on the table before me which contained several glasses and carafes. "Rogers, pour Mr. Forbes a drink."

Rogers stepped out of the shadows and said in a somber voice, "Orange juice or grapefruit juice, sir?"

I ordered the orange juice. Mrs. C then dismissed Rogers, who slunk out of the room.

"I understand you're a detective friend of Mayor Nye, stuck in town for a few days due to car trouble," she said.

"You seem to keep up with what's happening around Cordoba," I replied.

"I have my sources. Tell me, what do you think of our bustling metropolis?"

"It has a certain charm," I confessed, "but the pace is a little slow for me. But if I may remark, you seem a little out of place here also. You are a more worldly and cosmopolitan type than most of the people around here. What appeals to you about Cordoba?"

"I came here many years ago from San Francisco. My husband had passed away and my health was failing. My doctor at the time recommended a dry climate. I'm a private person and I could not find anyplace drier or further off the beaten path than Cordoba, so I settled here. I know the townspeople consider me arrogant and standoffish (again, I have my sources), but I like to think I've helped the town with contributions for some improvements. Unfortunately, my health continues to suffer."

Seeing an opening, I jumped in. "As a matter of fact, I visited Doc Fletcher this morning, and he mentioned that you were in last week."

"In a town this size, everybody knows pretty much everything about everybody else," snarled Mrs. Cavendish. "At least they think they do," she continued with a Cheshire cat smile.

"I'm sure Doc meant no harm. He seems like a nice fellow. I also admired his selection of magazines."

"His collection is impressive. Still, I wouldn't recommend it to anyone interested in current events."

"He mentioned that a few of his magazines had gone missing," I slipped in. "You noticed nothing unusual or suspicious while you were there, did you?"

"The only unusual behavior in that office would be if that receptionist of his had the common courtesy to offer a patient a cup of coffee while the doctor was busy gabbing in the back room and keeping paying customers waiting. And the only thing suspicious is their relationship. He's old enough to be her father. Besides, a few old magazines missing is not a big deal. And if you think I had anything to do with the disappearance, I resent the implication."

"No, I wasn't suggesting you were involved," I said, although her guilty tone gave me something to think about. "But those old magazines mean a lot to Doc, so if your sources hear of anything, please let me know. I'm staying over at the boardinghouse." I placed my glass back on the tray and got up to leave.

"I know where you are staying. And I will let you know if I hear anything. But I must warn you, in a small, isolated town like this, it is not wise, even for a man in your profession, to go around digging up dirt, unless you're helping Mr. Suarez find earthworms. Mr. Forbes, you seem like a perceptive fellow, but you may find I am not the ogre that the citizens of Cordoba think I am." The Cheshire cat smile appeared again as the rest of her disappeared into the chair.

When I stepped into the hall, the butler was waiting. "I'll show you out, sir," he intoned.

"Don't bother, Rochester, I can find the way," I said as I headed into the relative coolness of the ninety-degree day outside.

CHAPTER 11

THE SECOND AFTERNOON

As I strolled along, I forgot about the enigma that was Mrs. Cavendish and thought about my next steps. Maybe pay a visit to Indian Charlie. Plus, I wanted to get a better look around the outside of the diner. I decided to stop by and have a talk with Hilda Bluff.

On the way, I stopped to visit the Flagg sisters. Mabel and Jewell were home, but Ruth, who was sitting next to Mabel on the swing, was somewhere in the heart of Africa, staring down a charging rhino with Clark Gable.

After a short visit, I gave my regards to the sisters and headed over to the diner. The place was empty except for Hilda, who was sitting at the end of the counter reading a magazine. She got up when I entered and stepped behind the counter. I walked over to the left toward where she had been sitting and took a seat, glancing at the magazine she left sitting on the counter, just in case. However, this magazine was one of those celebrity gossip magazines and was of more recent vintage than the ones Doc had lost, but not by much, judging by the pictures of Britney Spears and Madonna on the cover.

Hilda wandered over and said, "Hello, Milo. It's a little too early to find Ben here. I don't think he's finished his morning nap yet. What can I get for you?"

"Just a cup of coffee." I was still working off Felicity's breakfast. "I'll catch up with Ben later. Besides, I wanted to have a conversation with you about the shady figure that's been hanging around."

I studied Hilda as she got the coffee. She was a large woman in girth, but the face did not have the usual pudginess of a woman her size—sort of like when you blow up a balloon and one half fills up with air before the other. She wore heavy makeup and lipstick and had blond, curly hair in a Shirley Temple cut. The hair was either dyed or a wig since I detected some darker hairs around the edges. Her voice was high and squeaky when she spoke.

"Not much I can tell you," Hilda said as she set down the coffee. "Frank has seen him once around midnight before he went to bed, and I heard noises in the middle of the night one time. I got up and looked out the window and saw movement but couldn't make out any details other than that the prowler appeared to be large. Whether he has been snooping around on any other nights, I couldn't tell you."

"Okay, I'd like to look around back later if you don't mind, see if I can find anything."

"Help yourself," Hilda offered. "There's nothing much back there but some garbage cans and the old water tank and heater that used to supply water to the diner."

"It won't disturb Frank if I go poking around out there?"

"Oh, no. He sleeps all day and then takes the night shift."

"That's quite an arrangement you two have." I wanted to find out more about their relationship but didn't want to appear to be prying. "How long have you owned the diner?"

"We've owned this thing forever. We bought it in New Jersey and ran the diner in Secaucus for many years. When Frank's health deteriorated, and the neighborhood followed, we decided to move to a healthier climate." It seems everybody came to Cordoba for the climate. "So we hitched up the diner and headed west, traveled Route 66 and ended up here, bought the house out back and settled in.

"In Secaucus, we used to run the diner together but were always fighting and getting under each other's skin, so Frank got the idea while driving out here to open the diner up as a bar in the evening. I run the diner during the day, and he runs the bar at night. We each keep our own profits, and we only see each other in passing. We eat a quick dinner together between shifts, but I'm in bed by the time Frank closes the tavern, and he's sleeping when I come down here in the morning. We seem to get along better with those arrangements." Hilda winked.

Hilda asked about my life, and I told her about living in San Diego and enthralled her with the many baffling mysteries I had been involved with, including the case of the missing dog and the mysterious disappearance of the six of hearts from my deck of cards. By that time, I had finished my coffee and told Hilda I would have a look around.

I left the diner, turned left, and proceeded down the sidewalk to the end of the diner, looking for any signs of disturbance along the way. In the dry dirt of the desert, there was little chance of finding footprints. I wondered where Sam had located some. At the end of the diner, I took another left and walked along a gravel pathway that ran along the side of the diner. The gravel went all the way to the end of the street and may have been intended to be a primitive parking lot before Frank and Hilda realized there were few cars in Cordoba, and those were only used to go to faraway places like Bell City and Chiquita.

Again finding nothing, I made another left and headed around back. There I came across the water tank, which was about five feet high and about four feet across. The tank was covered in rust and had obviously not been used in several years. The pipes that connected the tank to the diner were lying in a pile next to the tank. There was a door near the bottom I assumed was used to add coal or wood to heat the water. The door was rusted shut.

The garbage cans were some distance down, next to the back door of the diner. They were battered and dented, and there was nothing remarkable about them.

I turned and directed my attention to the yard leading down to the house. There were several windows in the back of the house that looks out on the diner.

Below Frank's house, I could see the Flagg sisters' house on the other side of the street. It looked like they had a clear view of the diner from their upstairs windows. I thought I saw the glint from the telescope lens in the attic window.

At the top of the slope and close to the back door of the diner was a small vegetable patch that was evidently used to grow vegetables for the diner. There were a few tomatoes and cucumbers struggling to survive in the desert dirt, although the ground was well watered by a garden hose connected to a spout on the back of

the diner. As I looked through the garden, I thought I noticed footprints around a smashed tomato. The prints looked like they had
been there awhile and must have been the prints Sam was referring to. I had to agree with Sam that the prints were made by a
man's shoes.

I peered under the diner, which was raised about two feet off
the ground by wooden blocks. There could have been something
hidden in the dark areas, but I was in no mood to crawl underneath to find out. I completed my circuit, finding nothing else of
interest, and entered the diner again. Hilda placed another cup of
coffee before me without asking and said, "Find anything?"

"Not much," I replied. "I noticed your little garden in the back.
There were footprints in the middle."

"Yes, Sam pointed them out. They don't belong to Frank or me.
The prints are too big, and we walk around the outside so as not
to disturb the vegetables. The garden is small enough so we can
reach just about anything from the edges."

"When do you water it?"

"In the morning before work, but the water evaporates during
the heat of the day, so Frank will give it more water when he
leaves the tavern."

"What time does he close up?"

"Whenever the last customer leaves, around nine-thirty or ten,
though sometimes Lucky will stay late and fill Frank's head with
dreams of finding his gold mine. Frank seems to believe the stories. I even saw him driving out to the desert early in the morning
last week. He threw a shovel and a sack in the pickup, drove off,
and came back a couple hours later."

Getting back to the garden, I said to Hilda, "If those footprints
don't belong to you or Frank, they may be the intruder's. He
would be unfamiliar with the back of the diner and may have
stumbled into the garden while searching for something. But
what? There's nothing but garbage and the rusted tank out there,
and they don't seem to have been disturbed. I take it by the looks
that the tank is no longer in use."

"No, that hasn't been used since we moved from New Jersey.
When the diner was first built, the tank was used to provide hot
water. Water was pumped in the top part, and coal was burned in

the bottom to heat the water. This was replaced by a more sophis-
ticated system. We thought of leaving the tank in New Jersey
when we left, but the town of Secaucus threatened to charge us to
remove it, so we threw it in the diner when we left and took it out
when we got here."

"Well, the other option, if he wasn't interested in anything
around the diner, is that he was trying to gain access to the inside
of the diner or to the back of your house. Anything peculiar happened around there lately?"

"Not a thing. I don't know why anyone would go snooping
around our house. We live quiet lives and don't have enough
money or belongings to attract thieves."

At that point, Ben walked in and Hilda wandered off to get him
a cup of coffee.

Ben sat down next to me. As we began to talk, Phil Childers entered and sat next to Ben.

"Before I forget," said Phil, "Sam asked me to tell you to stop at
the store so she can update you on her investigations. Have you
and the junior detective made any progress yet?"

"Not much," I said. "I spent time looking around the back of the
diner but didn't see much."

"Sam says you're also onto the case of the purloined periodi-
cals."

"Yes, Doc is missing a few magazines from his collection."

"Oh well, our little problems are not that important," said Ben.
"Why don't you relax and enjoy the rest of your visit?"

"The snooper around the diner is probably nothing, but I'd like
to help Doc if I can. I think I'll run out and see Indian Charlie this
afternoon. He was in Doc's office the day the magazines went
missing. You know, there used to be a pretty good racehorse
named Indian Charlie."

"I don't think this is the same Indian Charlie," said Ben with a
straight face. "He's fast but he's not that fast."

"Stepping on cactus all the time has slowed him down some,"
added Phil.

I didn't laugh since I wasn't sure if they were joking.

Ben said, "You can take my car again. The ranch is about three
miles out of town to the west." He gave me directions to the ranch.

"How's your car coming along?" Phil asked.

"Maybe I'll take another trip into Bell City later to check on it. Not that I'm anxious to leave town," I joked.

"No offense taken," Ben said. "Visitors never seem to stay long in Cordoba for some reason."

"That Mr. Costello has been here a week or two," said Phil. "If you're asking me, he's behind any funny doings in town. Why would he hang around for so long?"

"For one thing, he likes Felicity's cooking," I said.

"That's just what I've been telling you," said Ben. "Stay around long enough and you'll never want to leave."

"I don't think I've reached that point yet, but the town does sort of grow on you. I guess I'll be off to see Sam and pay a visit to Indian Charlie."

"Car's parked in the same place. Keys are in the ignition," Ben hollered as I left. "And watch your step when you get out to Indian Charlie's. Oh, and don't forget the fair this afternoon."

I assured Ben I would be back in plenty of time and headed out.

CHAPTER 12

INDIAN CHARLIE

I walked across to the general store and stopped to see Sam. When she saw me, she said, "I checked out the magazines at the boardinghouse, but none of them matched the missing ones. I asked Aunt Felicity if Mr. Costello had been reading a lot, and she said he only reads a newspaper that was sitting on the table. It was called the *Daily Racing Form,* and it had a lot of strange names in it, and a few of the names were circled. I figure it was some sort of code, but I didn't want to take the paper since it might look suspicious, and besides, it's not mine."

"That's okay. It's probably nothing. I'm heading out to Indian Charlie's place to talk to him."

"What do you want me to do?"

"You can take the afternoon off."

"Thanks. Maybe I'll tail Mr. Costello again, or that creepy lightning rod salesman."

"Okay, but don't make a pest of yourself."

I found Indian Charlie's ranch without much trouble. The midday heat was uncomfortable, especially since the air-conditioning in Ben's car didn't work. I was forced to leave the windows open, and by the time I arrived at the farm, both the car and I were covered in dirt and dust. To be fair, the car was already in that condition when I took off, but that didn't make me feel any better.

The farm consisted of a few acres covered by small cacti growing in rows. There was a small wood-frame house in the back I assumed was Indian Charlie's residence and a good-sized toolshed. A little way down the rows, I saw Fred Dobbs hoeing a row, and a little further on, another man was bent over a cactus. I walked over to Dobbs.

"Hello, Kid, how's it going?"

"Hello, Milo. Didn't expect to see you out here. Sorry if I made a nuisance of myself last night."

"Not at all. I enjoyed the company. Do you work out here much?"

"Whenever Indian Charlie needs me. I also work jobs around town. I keep up the grounds for Miss Felicity for my board. Sometimes I do work for Mrs. C that her man can't handle, cleaning out wasp nests and things like that. Are you here to see Charlie?"

"Yes."

"That's him over there."

"Thanks. I'll see you on the way out."

I walked over to Charlie, who stood up as I approached. He shook my hand when I introduced myself and said, "Do you want to buy a cactus?"

"I'm not in the market for any right now, but I'll keep you in mind."

He was well built and not tall and had the color and look of a Native American, with longish, straight black hair and black eyes. We walked along the rows as we talked, and every so often he would stop and stoop and inspect a cactus. He had a slight limp, which I guess was an occupational hazard. As we talked, I discovered he was well-spoken and intelligent.

"People come out here sometimes and expect to have a powwow with a tribal chief. They seem somehow disappointed when I mention my botanical degree from Stanford."

"I'm impressed. How did you end up out here?"

"I lived on a reservation across the border in Nevada, then worked my way through college and had a job doing botanical research, but after a while I became tired of living with all the well-intentioned people, and some not so pleasant, who perpetuate the stereotypes of the Native American, so I came back here. I wanted to work with the land, but not much grows in these parts. Not even the cactus grows to full height, so I grow small ones for houseplants. Besides, the weather around here suits me."

"For all the dry, hot, dusty weather I've endured since I've been here, it seems like half the population of Cordoba has come here for the climate."

Indian Charlie laughed. "At least we know what to wear every day without looking out the window in the morning. But you didn't come out here to discuss the weather. What can I do for you?"

I explained about the magazines that went missing the day of his visit to the Doc.

"Did you see anything unusual while you were there?" I asked.

"Is that a polite way of asking if I took them?" He smiled. "No, Doc's magazines aren't the type of reading I enjoy. I use the library at the boardinghouse. If Felicity should ask about the copy of *Crime and Punishment* I borrowed last month, tell her I'm almost finished and will return it by next week. I'm sure there's a waiting list.

"But back to your question, I saw nothing unusual at Doc's office. The only other patient present when I was there was Mrs. Cavendish. She arrived after I did, but the Doc saw her before he saw me. This was not a slight on me but more of an acknowledgment of Mrs. C's status. She goes in before everyone in Cordoba. Leo gave me a slight smile of apology, but it was not necessary.

"I saw Mrs. C reading magazines, but I can't imagine her taking them, except maybe by mistake."

"Well, thanks anyway. It was nice to meet you, Charlie."

"Maybe I'll see you at the tavern sometime," Charlie said. "I stay away from the fire water, but Frank keeps a decent merlot he orders for me."

I said good-bye to the Kid on the way out and took a dusty ride back to town.

CHAPTER 13

TRAGEDY AT THE FAIR

I drove to Bell City to find out there had been no progress on my car. It was midafternoon by the time I got back to Cordoba. I dropped Ben's car off at the mayor's office and stopped in to talk to Ben. He said he would be leaving for the fair in about an hour and would pick me up at the boardinghouse.

I returned to the boardinghouse and took a bath to wash off the dust from my trip to the farm. I would have preferred a shower, but the bath was relaxing and gave me time to think about the mysteries and complexities of the town of Cordoba. Although I couldn't imagine living in this town for an extended period, I had to admit that in some ways, I was enjoying the relaxed pace of the place.

As I got out of the tub, the knob on the locked door turned.

"Be right out," I shouted. "I'm just finishing up."

"No rush," said the voice on the other side of the door, which I recognized as Costello's. "I can wait."

I wrapped a towel around myself and opened the door.

"It's all yours," I said.

"Thanks. See you at supper."

I dressed and went downstairs and found Felicity sitting in the parlor. She was wearing a bright sundress, and her hair was tied back in a ponytail. She started to explain that she was also waiting for a ride to the fair when the front door burst open and Sam ran in.

"Here we are, Aunt Felicity!" Sam shouted.

"My ride's here," Felicity rose from the chair and headed to the door. "See you there."

"Do you need a ride, Milo?" Sam asked. "We can squeeze you in our car."

"No thanks, Sam," I replied. "Ben's giving me a ride."

I walked out to the porch with them and saw that the car was already full with Sam's parents, brother, and a scruffy-looking dog. Sam and Felicity squeezed in and waved as they left. I sat in a chair on the porch and waited for Ben.

About five minutes later Ben pulled up in front of the house. Phil was sitting in the passenger seat next to Ben. I headed for the car and took a seat in the back.

"Buckle up for fun," Phil half turned around and said.

I had no response to that comment, so Ben jumped in.

"The Tri-County Fair is the big event of the summer. Everybody in the surrounding area shows up."

"Yesterday, they had a miniature rodeo, only for the kids," Phil said. "They had to lasso little pigs that were let loose on the football field."

"That was a hoot," said Ben. "Today, there's a parachute jump."

"Not a pig, I hope," I said.

Ignoring the sarcasm, Ben continued. "No, Billy Webster from over in Bell City. But it still should be exciting."

Ben turned on Third Avenue and headed east out of town, heading in the opposite direction on the same road I used to get to Indian Charlie's. As we drove, Ben and Phil gave me the layout of the tri-county area. Cordoba is in Culver County and is the county seat by virtue of being the only town in the county. Bell City is in Bell County to the north of Cordoba, and to the east, where we were heading, is Chiquita County. Bell City, Chiquita, and Cordoba were the only towns of any size, if you call a population of seventy-three a size. There were several outlying areas where isolated populations lived and a few ghost towns in the desert.

Like the route to the cactus farm, the road quickly turned to dirt. Other than some small trees I couldn't identify and some cactus a little larger than Indian Charlie's, there wasn't much scenery. As we got further out of town, the land became hilly and sloped, but the features were the same, sort of like a carpet of the same material where a few dogs had crawled underneath.

After about a half hour, we reached a crossroads where another dirt road intersected the road we were traveling at a right angle. A rusty street sign on the intersecting road identified it as County Line Road. Another sign pointing in the direction we were traveling read "Chiquita 5 miles." We continued this road for another mile until we came to a large field on the left with a wooden fence in front. A little past it, I saw a stadium. To the right was a large parking lot, which wasn't really a parking lot but was just more desert where everyone was haphazardly parking their cars.

Ben eased his car into the lot and found a space about fifty yards back. We walked across the road to the fence, which announced we had arrived at the Tri-County Fairgrounds. Like the parking lot, the fairground was more open desert, this time with a fence in front of it.

Rather than just walk around the fence, which was no longer than fifty feet, Ben walked up to a ticket booth in the middle and asked for three adult tickets.

The ticket taker was a middle-aged woman wearing a big smile and a T-shirt that read "Fairest of the Fair."

"A dollar fifty," the woman said, still smiling.

Ben paid, the woman ripped three orange tickets off a roll in front of her and gave them to Ben, Ben distributed the tickets, and the three of us entered the fairgrounds.

The entrance gave way to a midway, familiarly consisting of booths offering various games of chance alternating with booths offering fair food such as popcorn, hot dogs, and funnel cake. To the back and to the left of the midway were several small rides, including a small Ferris wheel.

After a stroll down the midway, interrupted by several stops as Ben and Phil—I refrained—took turns throwing baseballs at milk bottles and shooting little popguns at tin rabbits revolving around the back of the booth, Ben and Phil grabbed a hot dog. Again, I refrained. We then walked around the fairgrounds for a while. Ben introduced me to some locals, but I didn't recognize anyone until Sam ran up and grabbed my hand to pull me in the direction of her family. Phil and Ben headed back to the midway for more fun.

Sam took me over and introduced me to her parents, Bert and Millie, who were talking to Felicity. She then introduced her younger brother, Skipper, and her dog, Pard, the scruffy mutt I had seen in the car. By the looks of Skipper's blue lips, he was either freezing to death in the desert heat or he had visited the cotton candy booth on the midway. I deduced that cotton candy was the culprit.

While Sam and Skipper had a somewhat heated discussion about whether to hit the merry-go-round or the whip next, Bert, who had the family's red hair, a shade somewhere between Sam's and Felicity's, said, "We're heading over to the stadium to catch the parachute drop. Care to join us?"

"Sure," I replied. *I could use an excuse to sit down,* I thought. "I'll grab Ben and Phil and meet you over there."

"Will you be able to find them in the crowd?" Felicity asked.

"Don't worry, I know where to look," I said, turning toward the hot dog stand.

Ben, Phil, and I headed for the stadium while they munched on their hot dogs. Along the way, Ben pointed out various people he was familiar with. He motioned toward two men talking to each other near the entrance to the stadium, which faced the fairgrounds. One was wearing a police officer uniform a size or two too small for his belly. The other wore jeans, a plaid shirt, and cowboy boots and hat.

"The one in uniform is Chief Baker, the Bell City police chief. The man with him is the sheriff of Chiquita, Jim Turner."

We bypassed them and entered the stadium, which a sign identified as the home of the Chiquita Scorpions. Inside was a football field that showed equal portions of grass and dirt, and bleacher seats on opposite sides. After locating the Fremonts we walked up several rows and sat on the bench in front of them. Felicity, Bert, and Millie had been joined by Doc and Leo. We said our hellos and I inquired about the kids.

"They stayed behind with the rides," Millie said. "We'll pick them up after."

A large circle had been drawn in chalk in the center of the field as a target for the parachutist. A local dignitary was standing in the circle with a microphone, introducing the parachute jump.

"Mayor of Chiquita," Ben said, and then pointing to a young woman a few rows in front of us, "and that's Annie Webster. Her husband, Billy, is the parachute jumper."

We waited a few minutes, chatting with the group behind us until the sound of a small plane was heard. A few cheers went up from the crowd as we all tried to spot the plane, which was not yet in view.

Far up in the sky, a one-propeller plane appeared, first as a dot and gradually becoming larger. The plane dropped altitude and flew several circles around the field to more cheers before ascending again and making its approach for the parachute drop.

Once the plane had reached altitude and was nearing the stadium, a small figure appeared in the door of the plane, lingered for a few seconds, then jumped. We watched with anticipation, waiting for the parachute to open, which it did after Billy had floated for a few seconds. He was still a small spot in the sky as he wrestled with the parachute to direct it to the landing spot.

After a few more seconds, it was clear that he was not going to make it to the intended target but was drifting to the west, away from the stadium and over the fairground. We turned around to keep him in view. As Billy continued to drift several hundred feet from the ground, the parachute gave way and separated from him. Billy began a free fall, and a collective gasp came from the crowd. As he fell, he put his arms straight out and opened his legs.

There was a moment of silence until he fell from view behind the stadium walls. He was now too far away for us to hear the sound when he hit the ground.

It was another moment before everyone sprang into action. Most of the men got up and headed for the exit, including our group. Ben turned around and said, "You ladies stay here. Doc, you better come with us."

As we were rushing from the stands, I heard Millie shout, "The kids!" and Millie, Bert, Felicity, and Leo hurried behind us to search for Sam and Skipper.

We ran out and headed toward the cars. I noticed that the fairgrounds had gone quiet and realized that the people on the fairgrounds had had a better view than we in the stadium as Billy traveled overhead.

Most of the men rushed to the parking lot and piled into cars Keystone Kop fashion, including Ben, Phil, Doc, and I, who jumped into Ben's car. I saw Chief Baker lead Annie Webster to his police cruiser and take off with the siren blaring as we all proceeded west to find the crash site.

It didn't take long. The body had landed just on the other side of the dirt road intersection we had passed on the way in.

By the time we arrived at the scene, several men had already reached Billy and were standing around the body, not sure of what to do. Ben and I cleared a path so Doc could get through.

Billy was lying face down in the same spread-eagle position we had seen as he fell. We rolled him over so Doc could examine him. After a moment spent checking for a pulse and signs of breathing, Doc said, "He's alive, barely."

By this time Annie had made her way to the front of the crowd. She screamed when she saw Billy and rushed forward. Jim Turner grabbed her with both hands and said, "Don't, Annie."

She shook loose, gave Jim a hateful look, and screamed, "Let go of me!" Jim let go but Annie stayed where she was.

By this time an ambulance had arrived from Chiquita, and the emergency technicians hurried over to get Billy on the stretcher and into the ambulance.

"Careful, boys," Doc instructed. "I think every bone in his body is broken."

When Billy was in the ambulance, Doc and Annie got in the back and the ambulance reversed its course and headed to Chiquita.

Chief Baker made a futile attempt to restore order and yelled above the crowd, "Everyone back away. This is a crime scene." After everyone had moved back about a step and a half, the chief motioned for Jim Turner and Ben to come over. Phil and I wandered over with Ben.

"I think it's clear that this was an accident," Chief Baker said, "but I better investigate anyway. I'll have some of my boys cordon off the area to maintain the integrity of the accident scene."

"It's a little late for that," said Jim, "and I'll lead the investigation since the accident happened in my jurisdiction."

"Sorry, boys, you're both wrong," Ben declared with a calm authority I hadn't seen before. He motioned toward the intersection and the street sign.

"He landed on the Cordoba side of County Line Road. That means he's in Culver County and that means it's Cordoba's investigation."

"But Billy's a citizen of Bell City," Chief Baker protested.

"But his intended landing spot was in Chiquita," protested Jim Turner.

Ben responded. "Say a fellow lives in Los Angeles and decides to take a trip to New York City. He jumps in his car and takes off, but before he can reach New York, he gets bumped off in Albuquerque. Who handles the murder investigation? The LAPD? The NYPD? No. The Albuquerque police investigate the crime. Well, Billy landed in Albuquerque, and we'll handle the investigation."

Chief Baker and Jim Turner were silent for a minute or two, trying to find a flaw in Ben's logic. Finally, Chief Baker responded, "But Cordoba doesn't even have a sheriff. Hasn't had one in years."

Ben responded quickly. "By a stroke of luck, I hired a sheriff this morning." He put his hand on my shoulder. "Meet Milo Forbes, my new sheriff, just arrived from San Diego."

The chief and Jim looked incredulously at me. I'm sure my dumbstruck look didn't help.

Before I could mutter anything, Chief Baker said as he stomped off, "Fine. It's just an accident anyway."

Jim said, "In that case, I'll get to town and check on Billy."

After they had left, Ben turned to me and said, "What do we do next, Sheriff?"

"You can cut the charade, Ben," I said, somewhat annoyed. "They've all left."

Ben smiled. "Let's get back to the fairground and make sure everyone's okay."

We drove back and found the group we had left behind. The Fremonts and Leo had found Sam and Skipper on the fairgrounds. They had been riding the whip when the accident occurred and saw nothing, Sam being busy screaming and Skipper trying to keep his cotton candy down.

Bert, Millie, Felicity, and the kids were heading toward the parking lot. Phil told Leo that Doc had gone to Chiquita with the ambulance, so she got into their car and drove to Chiquita to pick him up.

On our way to Ben's car, we saw a dusty pickup truck pull into the lot, now half empty, and Indian Charlie jumped out. "Look what I found," he said.

We looked in the back of the pickup, and there was Billy's parachute.

"I found it about a half mile from the body," Charlie said. "I waited to show it to you until Chief Baker left." His distaste for Chief Baker was obvious.

"Why wait?" asked Ben.

"I didn't want him to see this," Charlie responded. He pulled out the parachute and pointed to a spot on the leather harness that had held the parachute to Billy.

There were clear markings that the harness had been cut through with a knife.

CHAPTER 14

MAN WITH A BADGE

Ben instructed Charlie to drop the parachute off at the sheriff's office, and Ben, Phil, and I got in Ben's car and headed that way too. Most of the conversation centered on the events of the day, but there were periods of silence when the three of us tried to process the events in our heads.

When we got back to town, Ben dropped Phil off at the grocery store and Ben and I proceeded to the municipal building, where Indian Charlie was unloading the parachute from his pickup. He carried it into the sheriff's office and dumped it in a vacant corner. As he was leaving Ben said to him, "Thanks, Charlie. Keep what we saw our secret for a while."

"I won't say anything, Ben," replied Charlie. "I'll see you guys later."

Ben and I walked into his office, and he again motioned me to the chair opposite his desk as he took his seat.

"Thanks for not exposing my slight misstatement today, Milo. It would have been embarrassing."

"You're welcome, but I don't know whether I'd characterize it as a slight misstatement. And how long do you intend to keep up with it before you turn over the investigation?"

"That depends on you, Milo. I'd like to officially hire you as sheriff, if you are willing."

Before Ben could go any further, I stopped him.

"Are you crazy? I'm only here for a few days. And either Chief Baker or Jim Turner is better equipped to handle the inquiry. I don't want to get involved, so if you don't mind, I'll mind my own business and spend an uneventful few days in Cordoba until my car is ready, at which point I'll head back to San Diego."

"I understand, Milo. It was foolish of me to ask. But let me tell you why I did what I did back there. I was trying to keep both Chief Baker and Jim Turner out of the investigation since they both have a history with Billy Webster.

"Billy and Jim grew up together in Chiquita. Best friends, played on the football team together. Annie Lee was Jim's girl-friend back then. After high school, Jim joined the Air Force. Annie said she'd wait for him to return. After a few years, a girl gets lonely and Annie started seeing Billy. First word Jim got of it was when he got the wedding invitation in the mail.

Needless to say, Jim was not happy. When he got back about three years ago, he had an angry confrontation with Billy and An-nie, and he hasn't spoken to either since. He settled back in Chiquita and became sheriff last year.

"Billy and Annie moved to Bell City, partly to get away from Jim, I think. Billy got a job at the airport in Bell City. He always wanted to fly. He's been in and out of work with medical prob-lems, cancer, I think. Annie works as a waitress in a Bell City restaurant, so they make ends meet."

"What about Chief Baker?" I interrupted.

"Chief Baker is a loudmouth and a bully. He stays in office more by intimidation than by popularity. One night last year, he had too much to drink at the restaurant where Annie works and made a pass at her. Billy, who was there, decked the chief, knocked him out cold. The chief didn't arrest Billy due to embar-rassment, but ever since then he's been making Billy's life miserable, harassing him, traffic stops, things like that. Billy de-cided to run against Chief Baker for the sheriff's job next year, and there's a good chance he might win since Bell City is growing tired of the chief's antics.

"So you see, Milo, I don't think either of them would give the in-vestigation the time it deserves. Everyone likes Annie and I think Annie at least deserves closure. Besides, if this turns out to be more than an accident, as that parachute harness suggests, both Chief Baker and Jim could be considered suspects."

"I see your point, Ben, but I'm not qualified to be sheriff, and I'll only be here for a few days."

"You're as qualified as they are. All I ask is that you spend a little time while you're here looking into the matter. If you have nothing by the time your car is ready, I'll turn everything over to the state police."

"Well, I guess I can live with those terms. But it will cut into the time spent searching for the prowler and looking for Doc's magazines."

"Great," Ben replied quickly, fearful that I might change my mind. "Let me see here." He searched through the drawers in his desk.

After rooting around for a few seconds, he pulled out a wallet made of cheap plastic, unsuccessfully intended to look like leather. He opened it up and I saw a tin star with the word "Sheriff" imprinted on it pinned to one side of the wallet. The other side had a compartment with a plastic window. The compartment was empty.

Ben searched in another drawer and came out with a stack of cards held together with a rubber band. He pulled a card from the pile and grabbed a pen. The cards had writing on one side with some blank spaces for information to be added. He filled in the blanks, stuffed the card in the pocket of the wallet, and proudly handed it to me. I looked briefly at the badge and read the card.

This is to certify that Milo Forbes *has been appointed* Sheriff *of the town of* Cordoba, *county of* Culver, *State of* California.

Ben had signed and dated the card at the bottom. Noting the enthusiasm Ben showed in completing the card, and the general wording, I wondered how many he had distributed to the citizens of Cordoba. Did Phil have one appointing him general store owner?

"I better swear you in to make this official," Ben said, rising from his chair. I also stood up.

"I don't have a Bible in the office, so I'll replace it with another book," Ben continued.

Unfortunately, there did not seem to be any other books in Ben's office. After searching for a minute or two, Ben's eyes lit on the comic book he had been reading the previous afternoon.

"This will have to do," he said, picking up the comic book and solemnly holding it out in front of him. "Place your right hand on the Bi...*book* and raise your left hand and repeat after me."

Ignoring the *comic* tone of the proceedings, I did as instructed.

Ben intoned, "Do you, Milo Forbes, swear to perform the duties of sheriff of the town of Cordoba to the best of your abilities and to uphold the laws of the State of California?"

"I do," I responded, avoiding the temptation to add, "so help me, Archie."

"Good," said Ben. He handed me the comic book. "You can keep this as a souvenir. I've finished reading it. That Jughead is a real hoot."

He then led me to the sheriff's office, comic book in hand, so I could begin my new duties. I threw the book on the desk, and Ben and I went over to inspect the parachute. As Indian Charlie had pointed out, the leather strap had been cut or ripped through in an area behind a buckle that held the harness to the jumper's body. The parachute and harness were old, so it was difficult to determine if this was done deliberately or was the result of wear.

Ben and I examined the rest of the parachute, but since neither one of us had ever examined a parachute before and neither had any idea what to look for, the examination was quick and inconclusive.

"Do you think the chute has been cut?" Ben asked.

"It's hard to tell," I responded.

"What's your next step?"

Having no idea what my next step in the investigation would be, I responded, "Supper."

Ben agreed this was a good idea, and we both headed out into the heat.

When I reached the boardinghouse, Doc and Leo were standing in the hall preparing to leave.

"How's Billy?" I asked Doc.

"Never made it to the hospital. Died in the ambulance. The ambulance just turned around and took him to the coroner in Bell City."

"That's too bad. Did he say anything before he died?"

"No. He never regained consciousness. It's better that way."

"I guess maybe you're right," I said as Doc and Leo headed out the door.

CHAPTER 15

TUESDAY NIGHT AT THE BIJOU

D inner turned out to be hot open-faced sandwiches using the leftover pot roast from the previous evening.
Felicity explained that she had prepared something
quickly since it was Tuesday night, which was movie night in the
library. She had thought about canceling after the accident at the
fair but thought it was better to keep to the usual routine. This
would also give residents the chance to be together and talk
things out.

All four of her boarders were present. Most of the conversation
centered around the events at the fairground. Other than that,
there was little conversation, and everyone went their separate
ways after dinner. I again assisted with the dishes.

"You deserve a cut rate on the room for all the help you give
me," Felicity said.

"That's all right. If you hadn't noticed, I enjoy being around
you." I thought I saw her blush a little. "By the way, what is the
room rate? I forgot to ask."

"Don't worry," she said, smiling. "You can afford it, Sheriff."
News travels fast in Cordoba.

After cleaning up the dishes, we went to the parlor to prepare
for the movie. We turned the furniture around and pushed it toward the fireplace to make room for about a dozen folding metal
chairs which were lined in three rows facing the front of the building. I then helped Felicity set up the portable movie screen and
the projector in the rear of the room.

Since there was a little time before the first and only showing,
we returned to the dining room for a cup of coffee.

"Phil will be over in a little while with the film. He has a friend in Los Angeles who collects old films, and Phil borrows them so we can have a feature film every couple of weeks."

"I believe you said it's *The Big Sleep* tonight."

"Yes. It's one of Fred's favorite movies, although he has a little trouble following the storyline."

"He's not alone there. It would take a better detective than me to follow the plot of that movie."

Felicity laughed. "You're welcome to stay and watch. There's no charge, you know."

"Well, the price is right but no thanks. Watching an old film in the parlor is not my idea of lively Tuesday night."

Now Felicity turned angry. "You know, Milo, sometimes you infuriate me. You seem so nice but all the time I get the feeling you're laughing at the hicks of Cordoba behind our backs. I guess you'll be glad when your car is fixed, and you can get out of here. Well, don't worry, the town will survive just fine without you."

"I'm sorry," I apologized. "I didn't mean any disrespect, and you're right about the way I felt about Cordoba when I arrived. However, I think of the town in a different light since I've been here a few days. Everyone seems to get along with one another, and there's a quiet air of contentment among the citizens. I guess my big city rudeness still rears its ugly head every once in a while."

"All right, I forgive you. Come on in the kitchen and help me make the popcorn."

"You got it. And maybe I will stay for the movie."

The crowd arrived shortly thereafter. Most of the people I had already met or seen around town. Phil Childers arrived with the film, his wife Phyllis, and Ben Nye. Phil introduced me to Phyllis and headed to the projector to thread the film. Sam and her family showed up next, followed by Frank Blaine. He explained that he usually closed the tavern on movie nights so he could attend. Also, there was no business at the tavern with his regular customers attending the showing.

"We hear you're either keeping Sam out of trouble or getting her into it," said Bert. I learned that Bert was an elementary school teacher in Bell City, and Millie also worked part-time at the school.

Indian Charlie was the next to arrive, and he handed Felicity the copy of *Crime and Punishment* as he walked in. She feigned anger.

"It's about time," she said. "I was wondering if you were going to return it. What's next?"

"I'd like to read *Herodotus, The Histories* if you have a copy."

"I doubt it. But maybe I can pick up a copy at the Bell City library."

Indian Charlie thanked her and entered the parlor. Dobbs came downstairs and eagerly took a seat in the front row.

"A good chance for him to learn fresh dialogue, I guess," I said.

"Oh, he already knows it by heart, but he never misses a showing," said Felicity.

By that time all the seats were filled and several of the children were sitting on the floor in front of the screen.

"It looks like a good turnout," I said as Felicity and I passed out bowls of popcorn.

"Yes, there's normally a good crowd," Felicity replied. "Everybody in town has stopped in at one time or another—except for Mrs. Cavendish, that is. If there's a movie she's interested in, she borrows it from Phil and watches up in her house."

"She did seem quite standoffish."

"I think she's a nice person under the veneer. We have to find a way to let that person out."

By that time the movie was starting, and Felicity and I moved to the back of the room. She took a seat on an empty chair and I stood next to her. The picture was grainy but that didn't seem to bother anyone, including me. The sound was not of high quality but was enhanced by the voice of Fred Dobbs, who echoed the dialogue of every character.

I was just getting into the movie and taking mental notes on the way Bogie sweet-talked the owner of the bookstore across the street from the storefront he was watching. In my business, detective movies are instructional films, and besides, I knew a book owner I might like to try the lines on.

At that point, I heard footsteps coming down the staircase. I looked out the door on the right, which was ajar, and saw a shadow pass and leave through the front door.

Time to do some detective work of my own, I thought. I gave a quick look to Felicity, who had also seen the person leave. She gave me a slight nod.

I leaned over and whispered, "Flashlight?"

"In the drawer in the hall."

As I crept out of the room, she whispered, "Be careful."

CHAPTER 16

COSTELLO TAKES A WALK

S tanding on the porch, I saw Costello on the corner lighting a cigar. This would make it easier to follow him in the darkness, but the brightness of the desert stars and moon already provided enough light. Costello turned down Main Street and started in the direction of the diner. Along the way he stopped and took a puff on his cigar, which illuminated his face, giving it a devilish look. He continued walking until he came to the diner, which was unlit. After looking around for a minute, he took the gravel path that led to the back of the diner.

I kept a distance and used my experience to stay out of sight. Costello was gone for about five minutes before returning to the front of the diner. He then stood around for another minute and continued up Main Street before turning left at the next intersection.

I waited a few minutes for Costello to get down the street, then walked over to the diner, pulled out the flashlight, and searched the ground as I made my way to the back. I saw nothing unusual on my journey, and I was about to return to the front when the flashlight illuminated a pile of cigar ashes sitting at the base of the old water tank.

Upon closer inspection, I discovered that several screws had been loosened on the door at the bottom of the tank. I removed the screws without the use of a screwdriver, at which point the door fell loose, enabling me to peer inside. I shone the flashlight on the floor of the tank and then looked up the walls. The tank was empty. I wondered if it had been empty a few minutes earlier, or if Costello had removed the screws during his visit, removed something from inside, and replaced the door without bothering to tighten the screws.

Finding nothing else suspicious around back, I returned to Main Street and took the route that Costello had taken. When I reached the corner of Elm Street, I noticed the light on the Flagg sisters' porch was on and they were sitting in their assigned seats. Costello was seated in an Adirondack chair next to the swing and was talking with the sisters.

When he noticed me approaching, he waved his hand. "Hello, Forbes, or should I say Sheriff?" he said. "Had enough of the movie?"

"Yes," I said. "It looked like a nice night, so I thought I would take a walk around town."

"I had the same thought. I guess great minds think alike." Then he added, "Perhaps you should check the diner. As I was sitting here with the sisters, we thought we saw movement and a light, possibly a flashlight, out behind the diner. Didn't we, ladies? I notice you also have a flashlight."

The sisters nodded their assent in unison.

"Yes," I responded. "You never know when a flashlight might come in handy. Or, for that matter, a screwdriver."

With that, Costello got up to leave. As he passed me on the porch, he said, "I seem to see quite a bit of you around town, sort of like little Sam. As for me, I think I've had enough detective work for one night. I'll leave that to you. A man could get hurt if he gets too curious around the wrong people."

"Are you one of the wrong people, Costello?" I growled.

"Oh, heavens no," he replied. "I'm harmless, but I can't vouch for several other people in this town. Good night, ladies." And with that, he walked away.

I sat down in the chair Costello had vacated. I decided to avoid further embarrassment by not tailing Costello again.

"Would you like tea?" Ruth asked.

"We're all out of lemonade," said Mabel.

"But you can have some tea," added Jewell.

"No thanks," I said. "What do you think of Mr. Costello?"

"He seems like a nice man."

"But he seems a little scary at times."

"And he smokes a cigar."

I had to agree with Mabel on that one.

Changing the subject, I said, "Why aren't you ladies at the movies tonight?"

"We don't go out much."

"We prefer people to come to us."

"Once in a while, we attend if it's the kind of film we like."

"Like a musical."

"Or a comedy."

"Not gangster movies."

"I bet Mr. Costello likes gangster movies."

"I bet he does," I chimed in.

I nodded over at the house that Frank and Hilda shared and asked the sisters, "Do you ever see Frank and Hilda sitting on their porch?"

"Oh, no."

"They never sit on the porch."

"The only time we see them is when they walk back and forth to and from the diner."

"One comes up."

"A little while later one goes down."

"Sometimes we hear them talking or arguing."

"Not that we would snoop."

"Heavens to Betsy, no."

I thought maybe the telescope I had seen in the upstairs window was not for stargazing, so I said, "Have you seen anything unusual out back of the diner before the intruder you saw last week?"

"Nothing unusual," Ruth answered.

"How about Frank," Mabel chided Ruth.

"Yes, Frank was out the next morning," Jewell said.

"Before dawn, he took a sack and threw it in his truck and headed out of town," Ruth said.

"Passed right down the street headed for Chiquita," said Mabel.

"Not that we were snooping," said Jewell.

"Reminded me of the time I was stranded in the Petrified Forest," said Ruth.

With that, I knew I would get no more useful information, so I said, "Well, ladies, I better make my way back to the boardinghouse. I don't want to be walking the streets too late at night."

"Heavens to Betsy, no," the three said together as I left.

CHAPTER 17

DAY THREE

W hen I came downstairs the next morning, Costello was holding a copy of the racing form and talking to someone on the wall phone in the hall. The phone was one of the old types that had a dial rather than buttons. As I walked by, I overheard part of the conversation.

"Put a sawbuck on Foxtrot to win in the third at Gulfstream and another for I Love Lucy across the board in the fifth at Aqueduct."

Felicity was coming in the front door with the morning paper. I walked over and said, "I didn't know they made those things anymore," gesturing toward the phone.

"Oh, that's an old one. Hector is good at electronics and he rewired it or whatever you do to make it work with today's technology. There's another one like it installed in the diner. I'll go get breakfast ready."

"I'll help," I said.

We walked past Costello on our way to the kitchen; he was just hanging up the receiver. There was a little bowl on the table under the phone. Above the bowl was a handwritten sign taped to the wall which said, "A nickel per call, please." There were a few coins in the bowl. Costello started to walk away and then noticed me looking at the bowl and put his hand in his pocket, pulled out a quarter, and threw it in the bowl.

I continued toward the kitchen. When I reached the door, I glanced behind me in time to see Costello retrieving his quarter and replacing it in his pocket.

Breakfast was sausage gravy over buttermilk biscuits. The three other boarders ate and left. Costello did not mention the previous night, nor did I.

After breakfast, Costello went upstairs and came down a few minutes later with an overnight bag and went outside. I watched through the front window as he got into his rental car and drove off. I decided that there was no sense tailing him further and decided I'd prefer coffee in the parlor with Felicity.

"Did Costello check out?" I asked Felicity as we settled in.

"No, he said he was taking a side trip and would be back in a day or two," Felicity responded. "How did it go last night?"

I filled her in on the details, leaving out the embarrassing parts.

"I have my suspicions about our Costello," I said.

"Maybe he was telling the truth about checking on the diner the same as you," Felicity said.

"I doubt it. The door on that water tank was undisturbed when I looked at it yesterday morning, so somebody tampered with it between then and last night. Seems logical that Costello did it while he was back there."

"I guess you're right. But why would anybody be concerned about the insides of a dirty old water tank?"

"Beats me. Maybe Lucky O'Leary was back there looking for the Lost Dutchman's gold."

Felicity laughed. "Just the same, please be careful when you're snooping around, and especially around Mr. Costello."

"Well, I believe you're starting to worry about me a little bit."

"Of course I am." Felicity smiled. "I can't afford to lose a good boarder. And do you know how hard it is to get bloodstains out of a carpet?"

"I still can't figure out what Costello, or whoever he is, is looking for. Frank and Hilda don't seem to have anything valuable. By the way, they seem a strange couple. What's their relationship? Husband and wife? Brother and sister?"

"You mean you don't know?" Felicity asked, surprised.

"Know what?"

"For a private detective, you're not very observant."

"What do you mean?"

"Frank and Hilda are the same person."

"The same person?" I asked.

"Yes. Frank dresses up as Hilda during the day, putting on a fat suit and a dress and a lot of makeup, and runs the diner. At night he goes home and switches back to Frank and runs the tavern."

"No. I would have picked up on that."

"Think about it. Haven't you noticed the similar facial features? And nobody has ever seen the two of them together."

"I've never seen Martha Stewart and Fidel Castro together either," I came back, "but I'm pretty sure they're not the same person. And the Flagg sisters hear them talking and arguing. Not that they're snooping," I added.

"Others have heard them talking, but nobody has *seen* them talking. I think Frank has been doing this for so long that at some point, Hilda became a reality to him. Now, he is Hilda half the time."

"A split personality?"

"Sort of. But I think he started out that way as some sort of disguise. No one ever heard them talk to each other for the first year or so."

"Does anyone else in town know?"

"Everyone in town knows, except you."

"But why didn't anyone say anything?" I asked, embarrassed.

"There was nothing to say. To us, they are Frank and Hilda, two people just like anyone else in Cordoba. The way they do things, and why they do them, is their business, not ours, the same way nobody questions the way I run my boardinghouse or Phil runs his store."

"Well, I'll be," I laughed. "This is quite a town."

"That's what I've been telling you."

The front door opened and in walked Sam and Skipper, followed by Pard. Sam had her ever-present bag of peanuts, and Skipper was eating from a box of Dots, although by the way his jaw was working, you could tell that most of the candy never reached his stomach but was glued to various molars, incisors, and canines. Speaking of canines, Pard looked around for a minute, saw Felicity, and ran up for a pet.

"Hello, Pard," said Felicity. "How's my favorite pooch."

Pard turned and looked at me with an expression that said he wasn't sure what he was looking at, but he'd never seen it before. I recognized the expression since this is commonly how people look at me.

"Milo," said Sam, "I won't be able to help you today since I have to babysit Skipper. I promised Mom I would watch him this morning if she would drive me over to Bell City this afternoon."

"That's all right," I said. "Take the day off. What are you going to do in Bell City?"

"I want to do a little research at the Bell City library. Mom's having lunch with Dad while I'm at the library."

"Okay," I said. "And by the way, I think you should stay away from Mr. Costello for now. No more tail jobs."

Sam agreed and then Skipper broke in. "Do you have a gun?" he asked.

"No, I don't, Skipper," I said. "Why do you ask?"

"Mr. Costello says he has a gun," Skipper said. "I asked him and he said yes and patted his jacket pocket."

"Well, he was just kidding," I said, not with much certainty.

"I don't know. He looks like he would have a gun," said Skipper as he and Sam ran out the door, followed by Pard.

"Now I'm starting to worry," said Felicity. "Maybe I should ask Mr. Costello to leave."

"I wouldn't. He has done nothing, and he'll be easier to keep an eye on if he stays here. Any chance I could get a look at his room?"

"I don't think so. I always protect the privacy of my guests. As you say, he hasn't done anything."

"You're right," I said.

"However," Felicity continued, "this is the day I change the linens in the guest rooms. I guess it wouldn't do any harm if you want to help."

"I'd be happy to," I said, catching her meaning.

We headed upstairs, and Felicity grabbed a feather duster and some fresh linens from the hall closet and handed them to me.

Costello's room was unlocked, which was evidenced by the fact that the door, like the doors on all the other rooms, didn't have a

lock. The room was the same as mine, homey without much furniture. The one extra feature in his room was a roll-top desk in one
corner, with a matching chair.

I helped Felicity change the sheets on the bed, and while she
was dusting, I looked around.

I found a leather briefcase under the bed, but this was locked.
A battered suitcase in a corner of the room was also locked. Obviously, Costello was not a homebred Cordobian. Finding not much
of interest in the rest of the room, I turned my attention to the
desk. Some of the drawers had keyholes, but by now I was sure
that no key existed. I was correct and an inspection of the drawers
on the right side of the desk turned up nothing. The top left-hand
drawer held a copy of yesterday's *Daily Racing Form*. I inspected it
and found, as Sam had, that Costello had circled horses to bet on
for some of the races. Felicity looked over my shoulder as I inspected the racing form. The scent of her perfume made it difficult
for me to concentrate.

"He's not much at picking the horses," I said. "Some of his
picks are real nags and don't have a chance of placing. And who
was he placing bets with on the phone?"

"A better question is," Felicity added, "where did he get a current copy of the racing form? It's not the type of paper Phil sells at
the general store. Maybe the horses circled are some sort of code."

"Interesting, but I doubt it. We're getting a little carried away
here." I replaced the racing form in the drawer and opened the
drawer underneath. This was also empty except for one item—an
empty gun holster.

"Is that what I think it is?" asked Felicity.

"Yes," I responded.

"What kind of gun would fit in there?"

"Probably a .45," I said, since I think I heard that caliber mentioned on a TV detective show. I had no idea, but my vanity
required that I provide an answer.

I replaced the holster and rolled up the top of the desk.

The desk surface was empty as were all the various cubbyholes
except one, which contained some receipts: one was for a plane
ticket from Newark, New Jersey, to Las Vegas, and the other was
a receipt from a car rental company in Las Vegas. Both listed his

name as Carmine Costello with an address in Bayonne, New Jersey.

"Well, at least Costello is his real name," said Felicity.

"Not necessarily," I responded. "He could have used false identification for the plane and car. But the New Jersey address is interesting. That's where Frank Blaine came from."

As we left Costello's room, Felicity said, "Maybe you should confront him about the gun. You are the sheriff now."

"What for?" I responded. "That isn't illegal if he has a permit. And he hasn't broken any laws that we can prove. Better just keep our eyes on him."

Finding nothing else of interest, we continued to the other rooms, including mine, to change the rest of the linens. There was nothing of interest in any of these rooms, including mine.

CHAPTER 18

TROTZ FLYING ACADEMY

Deciding I better start earning my salary, assuming I was getting paid, I said good-bye to Felicity and walked over to the municipal building. Ben was not in his office and the rest of the building was empty, so I went to the sheriff's office. It was the same size as the mayor's office, with the main furnishings again being a desk and chair and accompanying visitor's chairs.

The one jail cell was in the back, and I was relieved to see there was a key to the cell—to my knowledge, the one and only key in the town of Cordoba—hanging next to the cell door.

I examined the drawers to the desk and found only an old roadmap of the surrounding area, a few pencils, and a small note-pad that had the name *Harry's Service Station* printed on the top along with Harry's Bell City address.

On top of the desk was a small calendar made of cardboard, also from Harry's Service Station, which would prove useful if a time machine appeared and transported me five years into the past.

Finding nothing else interesting in the office, I turned my attention to the parachute lying in the corner, concentrating my inspection on the area that appeared to have been tampered with. To my untrained eye, it appeared that the harness may have been cut through, but it could have just been natural wear. Upon closer inspection, I noticed several small holes on both sides of the area where the harness was ripped.

As I was deciding what to do next, I heard the front door open and Ben appeared in the doorway.

"Hard at work, I see," he said. "I stopped in to take care of some official business before heading over to the diner."

There was no need to ask what the official business was, since I saw a new comic book sticking out from his coat pocket.

"Do you mind if I borrow your car again?" I asked. "I'd like to take a drive over to Bell City and see some people." I was sure the sheriff's job did not come with a police car.

"Sure, go ahead," said Ben.

"Thanks. And maybe you can give me some directions. How do I get to the airport?"

Ben grabbed the pad and a pencil from the desk and drew a crude map as he gave me the instructions.

"How about the medical examiner?" I continued.

"His office is in the hospital." Ben ripped off the first page and drew another map.

I asked Ben if he knew Annie Webster's address.

"I don't, but I can get it for you," Ben said, motioning for me to follow him to his office. He pulled a yellow phone directory from his desk drawer. The cover had *Bell City—Cordoba—Chiquita* printed in large letters on the front and looked to be about twenty pages thick.

Ben copied the address to the Webster residence on a pad from his desk. His pad was also from Harry's Service Station.

I said good-bye to Ben and went back to the sheriff's office. I grabbed the parachute, threw it in the trunk of Ben's car, and headed to Bell City.

About twenty minutes later I pulled into the parking lot of the Trotz Flying Academy, on the outskirts of Bell City. The Academy consisted of one hangar with a small office attached. A short, paved runway was positioned next to the hangar. Through the open door, I could see a single small, one-propeller plane. I assumed it was the one that dropped Billy at the fair.

The sun was doing its usual job of frying everything in its path as I got out of the car and headed to the office, which was no cooler than the temperature outside. I wondered if folks in these parts were aware that a thing called air-conditioning had been invented.

The office of the Trotz Flying Academy was similar in size and appearance to Hector Suarez's office at the gas station, except for a lack of worms. The man sitting behind the desk was much older than Hector but had the same paucity of teeth. He had a few strands of wispy gray hair, and when he stood up, he had a slumped-over appearance.

"Mr. Trotz?" I asked as I entered.

"That's me," he responded. "Harold Trotz at your service, but everyone calls me Turkey, as in Turkey Trotz. Get it?"

I assured him I did. "My name is Milo Forbes and I'm the sheriff in Cordoba."

"Didn't know Cordoba had a sheriff," Turkey interrupted.

"It's only temporary," I said, keeping to myself that I would resign my position and be out of town as soon as my car was ready to go. "I'm investigating the Billy Webster accident."

"Terrible, terrible. Billy was a nice kid. Can't figure out what might have gone wrong."

"Were you flying the plane?"

"Yup. Not too many people around here can fly a plane. Jim Turner from over in Chiquita is the only person in the area besides me that has a pilot's license."

I ignored the fact that the flying academy didn't seem too successful. "Did you notice anything unusual or out of the ordinary about Billy yesterday?"

"Nope. As a matter of fact, he was in a better mood than I've seen him in for a while. He's had medical problems but said he was doing better."

"What type of problems?"

"Cancer, I think, but he didn't talk about it much. Lost his hair for a while. I figured it musta been that hemotherapy doin' it."

"Did you inspect the parachute before Billy's dive?"

"Nope. That's Billy's job and he always checked it out thoroughly before jumping."

"Did anyone else have access to the parachute?"

"It sits on a shelf over there, so anyone who was in the hangar would have access, but we don't get many visitors out here. Jim Turner was in a few days ago to go for a spin."

"Anyone else in the last week?"

"Only Chief Baker. He comes out just to harass me. Always threatens to close me down if I don't vote for him. He came in to check out the plane before the flight to make sure it was safe; like he would know what he was looking at."

"Let me show you something." I led Turkey out to the car, opened the trunk, and pointed out the rip in the harness.

Turkey whistled. "Looks like this has been cut partway through. See, the edges of the rip are smooth till you get to the top and then it looks more like a tear." He looked closer and pointed to the sides of the harness where the tear was located.

"Look here," he said. "There's some tiny holes punched on both sides of the tear, and it looks like pieces of ripcord material stuck in one of the holes."

"What do you make of it?" I asked.

"Don't know, but it almost looks like someone cut the harness most of the way through, then tied it together loosely with some rip cord."

"What would that do?"

"Don't know. My guess would be the harness would hold together, but once Billy jumped, the force of the descent and Billy's movements might cause the harness to rip the rest of the way."

"Would this cause the harness to fall away?"

"Don't know, but it might."

"One last question. I'm aware that you don't know, but wouldn't Billy have noticed this when he inspected the parachute?"

"As you say, I don't know, but it looks like the sort of thing Billy would notice, even though it was hidden under the buckle. Unless he was distracted or wasn't thinking clearly. Which reminds me. Come with me."

I closed the trunk and followed Turkey back to his office. He reached in his desk, pulled out a hypodermic syringe, and placed it on the desk.

"I found this in the back of the plane after the flight yesterday. I was going to give it to Chief Baker, but Billy was a good kid and I didn't want his name mixed up with drugs. Besides, I halfway suspect Chief Baker planted it to incriminate Billy when he inspected my plane. There was no love lost between those two."

"Do you have a bag I can put this in?" I asked.

"Only bag I got is my lunch bag, but you're welcome to it." He pulled a sandwich out of a small brown paper lunch bag and handed it to me. I lifted the syringe and placed it in the bag. At this point, I was worried more about my safety than evidence contamination since Turkey's greasy fingerprints were noticeable on the syringe.

"Thanks for your help," I said as I headed back to the car, "and please don't mention the needle or the parachute to anyone."

"You're welcome, young man. My lips are sealed." Turkey made an imaginary zipper movement across his lips. "I liked Billy. Hope you get to the bottom of this."

I was only hoping that my car was ready to go when I stopped at Harry's later.

CHAPTER 19

A TRIP TO THE HOSPITAL

B ell City General Hospital is a three-story brick structure a block off the main road, which continued to be called Main Street.

The medical examiner's office was on the second floor in the rear. The name on the door read Philip Baker, MD. Any doubts about whether he was related to Chief Baker were eliminated by a photograph of the two of them posing for a picture on the golf course. The family features also shone through in the pug nose and crew cut.

After I introduced myself and Dr. Baker checked my credentials, I said, "I see you know Chief Baker."

"He's my brother," Dr. Baker responded brusquely.

I then asked him if he had examined Billy Webster's body.

"My preliminary examination is completed," said the doctor. "I'm afraid we don't have the staff and resources to do things as quickly as they do in the city."

"Did you find anything in the initial exam?"

"No bullet holes or anything like that, if that's what you mean," he said, with more than a hint of sarcasm. "All indications are that Billy died from the impact when he hit the ground. I found nothing unusual in the condition of the body."

"Will you be doing an autopsy to confirm the cause of death?"

"I don't think that will be necessary considering the circumstances. And as I said, we don't have the resources."

I thought about telling Dr. Baker that he may want to do a toxicology report based on the syringe that was found in the plane. I decided against this, as I didn't think that would spur Dr. Baker to action, and I didn't want word of my evidence getting back to Chief Baker.

The heat felt even more intense as I exited the hospital. I realized that it was the first air-conditioned building I had been in since I arrived in Cordoba. But then again, I wasn't sure if that was air-conditioning or the coolness Dr. Baker had displayed toward me.

My next stop was Harry's Service Station on Main Street. When I arrived, I noticed that my car was up on the rack and a mechanic was working underneath.

I walked into the office, which was decorated with greasy handprints. Harry was behind the desk. I asked him if there was any progress on my car.

"Just a sec," he said, cigarette dangling from his lips, "I'll check with Chuck and see how it looks." He got up and headed to the repair shop. I watched through the window as he approached Chuck. They had a short conversation and Harry returned.

"May be done today, if not tomorrow or the next," said Harry. "Depends on if Chuck has any trouble getting the new axle in."

At least we were making progress. "Thanks," I said. "Keep me posted." As I walked out, I realized that during my entire visit, including the time Harry spent talking to Chuck, Harry had not once removed the smoking cigarette from his mouth.

CHAPTER 20

SAM ON THE CASE

It was now about noon, so I strolled down Main Street to find a place to eat. A few blocks down I came across the Bell City Public Library. I remembered that Sam had come to Bell City to do research this morning, so I stepped inside to find her.

There was a large circular front desk in the circular lobby. To one side against the wall, there were ancient-looking file cabinets, where I was sure for countless years Bell City and Cordoba students had waged a never-ending battle against the Dewey decimal system.

Branching off in several directions around the radius of the lobby were several rooms. Above each room, carved into the woodwork with elaborate lettering, was a description of the books contained therein. I started on the left. The first room was titled "Fiction". I peered in at the rows of books but decided this was not the place to find Sam. The carving above the second room said "Humanities." I wasn't sure what this meant, but I passed this room up also. I continued my circuitous route around the library.

The next room, toward the back, was titled "Research." I decided this was as good a place as any to start and walked in. There were several rows of books, and to one side there was a wall of microfilm in little boxes and machines which I gathered were used to view and print the microfilm. I headed in that direction, pulled out a box of microfilm, and read the label, which read, "New York Times, Oct. 1939–Feb. 1940." The boxes around it held earlier and later issues of the *Times* in sequential order.

Off the sides and back of the room were little alcoves with tables and chairs, where people could read with some privacy. I found Sam in one of these alcoves, looking over some documents on the table. To the side were two boxes of microfilm.

"How's the research coming?" I asked, startling Sam, who was deep in thought.

"Hi, Milo, what are you doing here?" she blurted.

"I came in to do a little research myself," I said. "How's your research coming?" I picked up the boxes of microfilm and saw they included film of the issues of *Look* and *TV Guide* from December 1954. "Still working on the magazine caper, I see."

"Yup, I thought if I looked at both, I might find some sort of connection."

"Good thinking. Any luck?"

"Well, I looked at all the articles and the only thing I could find was this." She picked up the papers on the desk, which were printouts of several pages of the magazines in black and white on glossy paper.

"Here, this picture was on the last page of the December 14, 1954 issue of *Look*."

The picture was titled "Derby Dolls" at the top and showed three women roller derby stars standing side by side, facing the camera with a roller derby arena in the background. All three were wearing the uniforms of their respective teams. The caption below read, "Three of roller derby's biggest stars in a rare moment of friendship. From left to right, Midge "Toughie" Brasuhn, Gerry Murray, and Penny Dreadful."

"Interesting, but what's the connection?" I asked.

"Here's an article from the *TV Guide* dated a week later," said Sam. "I couldn't print out the whole article because I ran out of nickels."

"Remind me to reimburse you for expenses," I said as I looked at the article. This one was titled "Roller Derby Rules the Airways" and concerned the ratings popularity of roller derby on television. It also profiled several of the star players with pictures of each.

"Interesting, but other than roller derby, what's the connection?" I asked.

"Well, the article mentions the three women in the *Look* picture. That's a connection, isn't it?"

"Yes, but how would it fit in? I doubt if any of our three suspects were too interested in the roller derby."

"Take a look at the picture again." Sam pulled the *Look* page from my hand and pointed at the third woman, the one named Penny Dreadful. "Doesn't that resemble Mrs. Cavendish? And she's old enough to be the right age."

"I guess it sort of resembles her," I said, unconvinced. "But what's your point?"

"Maybe Mrs. C was a roller derby star in the old days. She was looking through the magazines in Doc's waiting room and came across her pictures. She was worried that someone might see her picture and recognize her, and she would be embarrassed that she was in the roller derby, so she took the magazines."

"Interesting theory," I said. "But number one, we don't know that the woman in the pictures is Mrs. C. Number two, why would she be embarrassed? And number three, based on my experience, we'd have a hard time getting a search warrant for Mrs. C's place based on this evidence. So even if she has the magazines, there's no way to find them."

"I'll think of something," Sam said.

I was beginning to think she might.

CHAPTER 21

ANNIE WEBSTER

Annie Webster lived in a trailer park outside of town. Leaving Bell City and continuing on Main Street in the opposite direction from which I entered, I traveled about five miles, passing an occasional small house but not much else until arriving at the Shady Acres Trailer Park. If you think this sounds more like a cemetery than a trailer park, the Shady Acres Cemetery was right across the street.

I turned left and located Annie's double-wide at the back of the park. I knocked on the door and Annie answered within a minute. She was holding a small child and was followed by a shaggy white dog of medium size.

Annie opened the door and talked to me through the screen.

"Can I help you?" she asked uncertainly, the way you do when a stranger shows up at your door. You don't want to help this person you don't know, and you have no reason to, but you can't think of anything better to say.

"My name is Milo Forbes. I'm the new sheriff in Cordoba," I said. "How are you holding up?"

"All right, I guess," she said, but the dark circles and numb look in her eyes said otherwise. "Come on in."

She held the screen door and I followed her into the trailer. She turned and looked at me with some suspicion, and the baby and dog both stared at me with the same wary look.

"I saw you at the fair yesterday. I didn't know Cordoba had a sheriff," she said but she didn't ask for identification.

"I started yesterday. I'm very sorry for your loss."

"You picked a hell of a day to start," Annie said, half laughing and half crying. "Care for a cup of coffee?"

"If it's no trouble."

"I've got some brewing. I'll be right back."

Annie put the baby in the playpen and headed for the kitchen. She was a slight, pretty girl with short blond hair, darker at the roots. I guessed she was in her mid-twenties, though her weary appearance made her look older. I got the feeling that the numbness of her expression was not wholly caused by Billy's death but also from trying to survive in a harsh climate in a small town with few prospects.

The trailer was furnished cheaply, but the place was neat and clean. I took a seat at a small dining room table. The baby and the dog were still staring at me when Annie returned with the coffee.

"Milk or sugar?" she asked as she placed the mug in front of me.

"No thanks. Black is fine."

Before I could say anything, Annie said, "If you're here about Billy, I don't know how much I can help you. You saw as much as I did."

"Just tell me a little bit about Billy."

"Not much to tell. We both grew up in Chiquita. Got married after high school and moved to Bell City. Billy's had odd jobs to make a living. He worked at Harry's garage a little and over at the airport. I work as a waitress and we pretty much just manage—managed—to make ends meet." She broke down again.

"Had he been jumping long?"

"He's done it for years. Ever since we were in high school, he's always wanted to fly. Sort of captivated with the sky. I guess maybe that was my problem. Everyone I was involved with was more interested in the sky than staying grounded."

"Jim Turner too?"

She gave me an ironic look.

"Jim Turner too. Gossip travels fast in a small town," she said. "Jim and I were dating, and Billy and Jim were best friends. You've heard the story before. Star high school quarterback and running back, head cheerleader. That was Jim, Billy, and me. Jim went off to be a pilot. I told him I'd wait for him. You can imagine the rest of the story. I grew tired of waiting, and Billy had always had a crush on me.

"By the time Jim got out of the Air Force, Billy and I were married. There were the expected confrontation and angry words, but mostly Jim was just hurt. He never talked to either of us again unless he had to, and he avoided us whenever possible.

"After a while, it got so uncomfortable that Billy and I moved here to get away from Jim. I was caught in the middle. Jim hated me for marrying Billy, and Billy thought I was still in love with Jim."

"Were you?"

Annie looked at me and gave me a weary smile but didn't answer my question.

"I guess you might have been better off if Billy had joined the Air Force with Jim," I continued.

"Billy never wanted to fly a plane like Jim. Billy wanted to fly. He had an obsession with being able to soar like an eagle above the trees. That's why he took up parachute jumping. It was the closest he could get to flying."

"Jim flies at the airport, I understand."

"Yes, but the two always managed to avoid each other by checking the airport schedule."

"Did Billy have any other problems—alcohol, drugs?"

"He drank a few beers but no drugs I know of other than for his illness. Billy had some rare cancer of the bone. He was in bad shape for a couple of years. He had drug treatments then and chemotherapy and started getting better."

"How was he doing recently?"

"He'd been feeling a lot better. Last week he had a doctor's visit, and Dr. Cooper said the cancer was in remission. Billy's been a lot happier ever since—was happier, I mean."

"Anybody besides Jim that Billy didn't get along with?"

Annie's expression changed. "Why are you asking all these questions? Billy's death was an accident, wasn't it?"

"I have no reason to think differently," I lied, "but I want to cover all the bases, just to be sure."

Annie relaxed a little but remained on guard.

"Everybody liked Billy. He didn't make enemies."

"Chief Baker?"

"Everybody is Chief Baker's enemy. But he's more of a bully than anything else."

"Didn't Billy have a run-in with him, and didn't Billy threaten to run for police chief against Chief Baker?"

"Yes, Billy punched him when he made a pass at me, and Billy was going to run for chief. Do you think Chief Baker was somehow involved?"

"Not that I know of. Just gathering information."

"I guess you could put me on your suspect list too then. As I mentioned, Billy and I had our problems, but we loved each other. And Billy had a life insurance policy, but it's only for ten thousand dollars. Most of that will go for Billy's funeral. And I wouldn't do anything to hurt Billy Jr."

She picked up Billy Jr. from his playpen, where he was getting restless.

I had no more questions, so I also rose to leave.

"Come with me," Annie said suddenly. She walked to the kitchen with Billy Jr. in her arms.

I followed her and she pointed out a window over the kitchen sink.

"Look out the window and tell me what you see," she said.

I took a look. The trailer was in the back of the park, and the back window in the kitchen faced out into the desert with nothing in view as far as the eye could see.

"Not much," I said.

"Exactly," Annie replied. "Sometimes I stare out this window and think there's nothing here, and there's nothing in that direction or any other direction from this town. I don't even know what direction that is, but sometimes I think maybe I'll just go out the back door and start walking, and maybe in a few days or weeks, I'll end up in L.A. or Las Vegas. And then I realize that if I found someplace else out there, it would be another town just like Bell City, and I would be just as lonely there as I am here."

She turned away from the window and gave Billy Jr. a kiss on the forehead.

"Time for your nap, young man." She walked out of the kitchen with me close behind. "I hope I've given you what you needed," she said as she showed me out, "and thank you for showing an interest."

I told Annie I would let her know if I discovered anything and made a mental note to cross her off my suspect list.

CHAPTER 22

CHIEF BAKER

By now the afternoon was well shot. I decided to make one more stop on my way through town and have a talk with Chief Baker. Soon after reentering the city limits, I noticed a police cruiser following me. A short while later the red-and-blue lights started spinning, so I pulled over to the side of the road.

The cruiser pulled up behind me, and two uniformed policemen got out and came up to my window.

"Are you Forbes?" asked the older officer, who had a Chief Baker crew cut.

"Yes, I am."

"Chief Baker would like to have a talk with you down at the station."

I wondered how the chief knew I was in town. Then I remembered my conversation with his brother, Dr. Baker.

"Have I broken any laws?"

"No. Chief just wants to have a little chat with you."

"As a matter of fact, I was just on my way to the station to pay a call on Chief Baker."

"In that case, you can follow us in."

"No thanks," I told Crew Cut. "I've decided I don't want to talk to Chief Baker after all." I had decided that I wanted to speak to the chief on my terms, not his.

"I think it would be better if you came along. You don't want to get in trouble with the law," he responded.

"I'll be glad to go along if you want to arrest me," I said. "I'll step out of the car and you can search and cuff me. I've got a lawyer on retainer in San Diego who would like nothing better than to get some small-town yokel police chief in a courtroom and grill him about certain activities."

"We don't want any trouble," the second younger cop jumped in. "Chief just wanted to welcome you..."

"Shut up, Fred," Crew Cut interrupted. "I think we can persuade Forbes to come along."

"Are you crazy, Jake? We can't do this."

"Listen to Fred," I told Jake. "You've got two choices. You can arrest me and take me to the station, or you can get back in your car and drive off and we'll forget the whole thing. And by the way, it's *Sheriff* Forbes. What's it gonna be?"

Fred whispered something to Jake, who reluctantly turned away and headed back to his car. A minute later they drove off.

As I drove through Bell City, my anger was getting the best of me and I drove to the police station. I walked in and located the chief's office. He was seated behind his desk talking to Jake and Fred, who were standing on the other side.

"I see you changed your mind and decided to come in for a talk." He smiled.

"No. I stopped in to use the men's room. While I was here, I thought I would let you know that I don't appreciate your sending your men out to fetch me."

"Don't be offended," Chief Baker replied. "I wanted to welcome you to Bell City and see how your investigation was going."

"My investigation is going fine. If I need your help or think you need to be informed of anything, I'll let you know."

Chief Baker turned angry and said, "Listen, this is my town, and anything that goes on in this town is my business. You'll play ball with me or..."

"Your boy already tried that routine," I cut him off, motioning toward Jake. "This is my investigation and I'll handle it my way," getting angrier as I spoke, "and if you want to talk again, you can drag your lazy ass over to Cordoba. And the next time you talk to your brother, tell him to keep out of my investigation."

I walked out of his office as calmly as I could manage without looking back.

On the way out of the building, I stopped in the men's room.

CHAPTER 23

BACK IN CORDOBA

My first stop upon returning to Cordoba was the boardinghouse.

Felicity was outside, unloading groceries from the trunk of her car, so I gave her a hand. Frozen foods get unfrozen quickly in these parts, so speed is essential.

After we were done, we sat in the dining room with a glass of iced tea. I mentioned Sam's theory on the missing magazines to Felicity.

"That might not be such a farfetched idea as it sounds, Milo," she said. "Mrs. C is proud of her status as town matriarch. I'm sure she wouldn't like it if it became known she used to skate in the roller derby."

I told Felicity I remained doubtful and went over the reasons it would be difficult to investigate.

"I'll think of something," she responded. It seemed all the women in Cordoba wanted to be involved with this mystery.

I told Felicity that my car should be ready in a day or two.

"That's nice," she said, but she didn't sound like she thought it was nice at all.

I was beginning to think it wasn't so nice myself. I liked being around Felicity. Plus, there were certain matters I wanted to clear up before I left.

After getting everything put away, Felicity and I took a stroll down to see the Flagg sisters and deliver a couple of bags of lemons that Felicity had picked up for the ladies.

They were on their usual perch when we arrived, straining to reach the porch floor with their tiny legs so they could swing back and forth. I noticed that the swing was attached to its wooden frame by chains on both sides attached to hooks at the top. As the sisters got down from the swing to bring the lemons inside, I told them I could lower the seat by adjusting the links of the chain. This seemed to please the ladies, as they had never thought of that as an option.

"Thank you, dear, for bringing us our lemons," Ruth said to Felicity as they walked into the house.

"We couldn't make our lemonade without the lemons," said Mabel.

"You're our savior," said Jewell.

After I adjusted the swing and we had a short chat and the obligatory glass of lemonade, I said to Felicity, "Care for a cup of coffee?" She said yes, so we walked around the corner to the diner. It was again empty, except for Hilda.

"Hello, Hilda, how are you?" said Felicity as we entered.

"Well, if it isn't Nick and Nora Charles," exclaimed Hilda. "Care for a couple of martinis?"

"Leave the martinis to Frank," Felicity joked back. "I'll just have a coffee with cream and sugar."

"Care for a muffin or a piece of pie with that?"

"No thanks, just the coffee will do."

"And I'll have a black coffee," I added.

"Have a seat and I'll bring them over," Hilda said.

As I looked at her face, with the heavy makeup and wig, it now seemed obvious that it was Frank in disguise. She had the cups of coffee at the table almost before we arrived.

Felicity and I took a booth. "Well, I guess you'll be leaving soon now that your car is almost ready," Felicity began.

"Yes, I've enjoyed my little stay here more than I thought I would when I arrived."

"I hope I'm part of the reason for that," said Felicity.

"You are," I said, reaching out to take her hand from across the table. She didn't pull it away. "Still, I'm disappointed that I couldn't solve the town's little mysteries. I guess I gave everyone a bad impression of San Diego private detectives."

"Don't be silly. It was nice of you to offer to help."

I didn't mention I had sort of been roped in by the local residents.

"Anyway, I think I may hang around a day or two longer. There's nothing pressing in San Diego, and I hesitate to leave while Costello is still in town. Which reminds me, I should call my office phone and see if I have any messages. I'll be right back."

I walked over to the phone, which was attached to the wall between the restrooms. After some difficulty, I figured out how to access my voicemail and found as I suspected that all the messages were from bill collectors or salespeople. No requests for my services were included.

I returned to the booth and squeezed into my seat.

"Nothing that can't wait at home, so I guess you're stuck with me for a little longer."

"I'm not complaining," Felicity said. This time she grabbed my hand and I didn't pull away either.

By now it was midafternoon, so we headed back to the boardinghouse so Felicity could prepare supper. As we walked, I noticed a few grayish clouds overhead, the first clouds I had noticed since I'd been here.

"Do you get any rain at all around here?" I asked Felicity.

"Not often, but we get some. We have a rainy season that lasts for about a week."

When we arrived at the boardinghouse, Silas was standing on the porch also surveying the clouds.

"My senses tell me we're in for bad weather. I think I'll go over to the Cavendish place again and try to see if I can get in," he said.

"Don't bother," I said. "She won't see you."

"Nevertheless, I'll give it a try."

"Better take an umbrella. It looks like the weather is turning nasty," Felicity said. "There's one in the stand inside the door."

Silas went in, grabbed the umbrella, and took off.

Just as we walked in the door, the sky opened up and it began to pour.

Judging by the stillness inside the house, Costello was still out and so was the Kid.

"I hope the rain lets up before tonight. It's ladies' night at the boardinghouse, and all the girls are coming over for gossip and goodies. You're welcome to hang around, but it probably wouldn't interest you much."

"No thanks. I'll wander over to the tavern after dinner and hang out with the menfolk."

Since Costello would not be around for supper, cutting the food consumption by half, Felicity took it easy and just prepare sandwiches for dinner for whoever showed up. She decided to read and went to the parlor to grab a book.

I followed and sat down in an easy chair, picked up *Crime and Punishment*, and opened the book.

"On second thought," I said, getting up from the chair, "I think I'll head upstairs and take a nap. I'll sleep better up there."

CHAPTER 24

MEN'S NIGHT

T he nap was made pleasant by the sound of the rain on the roof above, which was heavy at times but slowed down intermittently. After an hour's rest, I got up and went downstairs. Felicity was now setting the dining room table for dinner. A loaf of bread had been placed on the table along with some sliced turkey and roast beef, lettuce and tomato slices, various condiments, and a large bag of potato chips.

She looked up as I entered and said, "How was the nap?"

"Fine." I eyed the spread on the table. "The patter of rain on the roof helped."

"I know it's not much of a supper," Felicity said, noting my glance, "but a cook needs a break. Besides, it will make the cleanup easier so I can finish before the girls arrive. It looks like the rain is letting up some, so girls' night is still on."

"I'm not complaining," I replied. "Everything looks good. I could also use an easier cleanup. I think I'm getting dishwasher hands."

Felicity laughed and turned to look as the front door opened. Silas and Fred walked in together. Silas closed the umbrella, shook it on the porch, and returned it to the umbrella stand. After they had dried off a little, we all sat down to dinner sans Costello, who had not returned.

Silas said he had gone to Mrs. C's house after he left us, but she had again refused to see him. While there he ran into the Kid, who was doing yard work for Mrs. C.

Fred said, "I take care of the lawn and do any repairs that need to be made. Rogers is getting on in years and can't handle the maintenance like he used to."

"That Rogers seems to be a stuffy gent," I said. "Where did Mrs. C find him?"

"He came with Mrs. C when she moved here from San Francisco. Working for her for so many years hasn't improved his disposition."

"What's the deal with her? She seems to lord it over the town."

Felicity replied, "When she came to Cordoba, she took the town under her wing, not that we needed it. She paid for some improvements such as sidewalk repair and new street signs."

"She had to replace the street signs, Felicity," Fred commented, "when she changed the name of Fifth Street to Fifth Avenue. The other signs had to be replaced to match her new one."

"Seems like she gets some preferential treatment around here," Silas said.

"I guess you could say that," Felicity replied, "but it doesn't hurt the rest of us any, and it seems to make her happy. No, I take it back. I don't think I've ever seen her—or Rogers—look happy. Satisfied, I guess, is a better description. I think if you can treat someone the way they want to be treated without causing yourself harm, why not do it."

"Makes sense, I guess," I said, digesting my sandwich as well as the conversation.

Dinner completed, Silas and the Kid headed out to walk to the diner. I told them I would see them there later and hung around to help with the cleanup.

The rain had let up and the ladies started arriving. I said hello to Millie Fremont, Phyllis Childers, and Leo, who arrived together. I noticed Leo was dressed a little more conservatively tonight, or maybe just more casual. No heels and gold glitter, just flats and flannel. Several other women I didn't recognize also arrived and Felicity introduced me to them.

"Get out of here and head down to the tavern so we can get started with the gossip," said Millie as she pushed me out the front door. "We'll help Felicity finish the cleanup."

"Tell Phil to take it easy with the beer," yelled Phyllis, who, like Phil, was jolly and round.

The rain had stopped, but there were still clouds above. The weather had cooled, and the walk to the tavern was pleasant. I arrived after Silas and the Kid. Silas was sitting on a stool in the middle of the bar, trying to convince a fellow I didn't recognize of the usefulness of a lightning rod, especially on nights like tonight. Fred was at the counter to the right, talking to Lucky O'Leary. Ben and Phil were in their normal spots. In the booth to the left of the entrance, Hector Suarez and Bert Fremont were playing a card game. All the cards were lying face down and jumbled up on the table between them. I stopped by on my way past to say hello.

"How's it going, guys?" I asked. "What are you playing?"

"It's called Scramble," said Bert. "All the cards are placed face-down on the table and mixed up. Each player flips over two cards and tries to match the same number or picture. If he matches, he gets to keep the cards. If not, he returns the cards facedown to the pile. Whoever ends up with the most matches wins."

"It looks like Hector has got you beat," I said, noting the difference in the size of their piles.

"Yeah, but when he turns over his cards, he flashes them quickly so it's hard to get a good look. And he slides the cards that don't match back into the middle of the pile so it's harder to remember where they are, rather than place them on top, like you are supposed to."

"Who says you are supposed to?" countered Hector in feigned anger. "Show me in the rulebook where it says you have to place the cards on top."

"I left my copy of Hoyle at home, so I guess I'll give you a pass," Bert countered with a smile.

Hector turned to me and said, "Harry at the repair shop called and said your car was done and ready to be picked up."

"Thanks," I said. "I'll run over in the morning and get it."

"I can give a lift if you like on my way to school," Bert said.

"Thanks."

"I'll pick you up about eight."

I continued to where Ben and Phil were sitting and took a stool next to Ben. I ordered a Somotha for variety. The two were watching the Padres game on a small black-and-white television sitting on a platform near the ceiling of the diner. Unless it was snowing in San Diego, the reception was lousy, and it was difficult to make out details.

The Padres were wearing their military uniforms with the camouflage shirts, and Ben and Phil were arguing.

"Why is a San Diego team wearing army uniforms?" Ben was saying. "San Diego is a navy town. Tell him, Milo," he said.

"That's right," I said. "I want to see them wearing dress blues."

"They wear the camouflage because it makes it difficult for the other team to see them," Phil said. "Watch that Padre on first base. He's going to steal second any minute."

Sure enough, the player broke for second on the next pitch and made it in standing, without a throw from the catcher.

"See what I mean?" said Phil. "The catcher couldn't see him down there at first base and forgot he was there."

"I don't know about the catcher, but with that picture," I said motioning to the TV, "I had difficulty seeing him."

"We don't get the best reception out here," said Phil.

"But it doesn't matter because we only pick up three stations anyway," Ben added.

From the other end of the bar, I heard the Kid, who was still talking to Lucky, exclaim, "Nobody puts nothin' over on Fred C. Dobbs."

"Look at that," Ben said. "He actually gets to be Fred C. Dobbs tonight. Lucky must be telling him tales of the gold he's going to find up in the hills."

"I guess you'll be leaving soon now that you have your jalopy back," Phil said.

"I might stay another day or two," I said. "I have a little business to clear up, which involves having a conversation with our friend Costello."

The diner door then opened, and Doc walked in. He said his hellos to everyone and took a seat next to Phil. He threw a dollar bill on the counter and ordered a drink from Frank. "Three fingers of redeye in a dirty glass, my good man, and leave out the little umbrella."

Frank drew a beer, plopped it down in front of Doc, and took the bill to an old-fashioned cash register at the end of the bar near where Doc was sitting. He pushed a few buttons and the cash drawer opened. He deposited the dollar and withdrew three quarters, putting them on the counter in front of Doc.

"I'll have another myself," said Phil, pushing his empty glass forward, "and put a little blood in this one."

Frank grabbed the glass and poured Phil another beer. He then reached under the counter and came up with a small can of tomato juice. He grabbed a can opener, opened the can, and poured a small amount of tomato juice into Phil's beer. After placing the remaining tomato juice in a small refrigerator, Frank took a quarter from the counter in front of Phil, leaving two quarters behind. I guessed this was either Phil's second beer or his sixth. Frank took the quarter to the register, put it on the counter, and picked up a small pad and pencil sitting on the cash drawer. He then scribbled something on the pad, ripped the piece of paper from the pad, picked up Phil's quarter, pushed a few more buttons, and deposited both the quarter and the paper into the cash drawer.

When he returned, Phil asked Frank, "What did you write on the paper you put in the register?"

"Oh, that," Frank said. "I had to put an IOU in the register for Hilda. The tomato juice belongs to her and the diner. She can get ugly if I take her stock and don't pay her back."

Changing the subject, Doc said, "Have you and your tiny Watson had any luck finding my magazines?"

"I'm afraid not, Doc," I said. "What can you tell me about the roller derby?"

Doc gave me a quizzical look, but answered, "I remember watching roller derby in the fifties when it was the big sport on television. Sports wasn't on TV much in those days, just roller derby and wrestling, and I think they were both fixed. Back then when television first started, there were only a few channels, and you had to watch on small sets with lousy reception."

"Thank heaven for today's technology!" Phil exclaimed, motioning at the TV above the counter.

Doc gave him a dirty look, then continued, "There was a professional roller derby league made up of teams from the major cities around the country. The game was played—and still is, although not as popular—on a round or oval wooden track, banked up the outside. Teams of men and women, wearing helmets, the women dressed in sort of Wonder Woman costumes, took turns skating around the rink for a minute or two at a time. There was one skater in the lead, and the objective of the other team was to have as many members pass that skater as possible, receiving a point for each member that made it. The other team would try to stop them from passing by blocking the lanes and elbowing anyone who tried to pass."

"Sort of like NASCAR without the cars," Phil jumped in again.

"Exactly," said Doc. "All the skaters adopted fake names and nicknames just like the wrestlers. Why do you ask?"

"Both of the issues that were taken from your waiting room contained articles about roller derby."

"That's good detective work," said Doc. I neglected to tell him that tiny Watson deserved the credit.

As we were talking, I noticed the Kid and Lucky O'Leary get up and leave together. A moment later we heard Lucky's Jeep start up and drive away.

"Looks like Lucky is taking the Kid out to his claim in the Sierra Madre," said Ben.

"Will Fred be safe out there?" I asked, concerned.

"He'll be fine," said Ben. "Either Lucky will drive him back or he'll spend the night up at Lucky's campsite. Lucky enjoys the company."

After a few more beers, the crowd in the tavern thinned out, and I decided to be part of the thinning process. As I got up to leave, Doc also got up and said, "I'll walk with you back to the boardinghouse. I have to pick up Leo on the way home."

As we walked, I said to Doc, "Are you familiar with Doctor Baker over in Bell City?"

"I've had a run-in or two with him. He's not much respected around here. Got his job as medical examiner and coroner because he's Chief Baker's brother, and nobody likes to cross Chief Baker. Why do you ask?"

"I talked to him today about Billy Webster's death, and he was evasive. He seems anxious to label the death an accident and close the case."

"Well, wasn't it an accident?"

"Probably, but I don't like certain aspects of the case, and the Chief and Doctor Baker don't seem to want me around. Turkey Trotz found a syringe in the plane yesterday after Billy jumped. I didn't want to turn it over to Doctor Baker, thinking it might get accidentally lost or be used to discredit Billy. Do you know anything about Billy Webster, whether he had a drug habit? Annie said he had a bout with cancer."

"No drugs as far as I know," Doc replied. "He has been fighting cancer for several years but seemed to be improving."

"Do you know his doctor? Maybe I should talk to him."

"Charlie Cooper. He's a good man, but he won't give you much information. He may maintain confidentiality even though Billy is dead."

"I thought he might be able to tell me if Billy was taking any medication through injection."

"I'll tell you what. Charlie is a friend of mine. If you like I can head over to Bell City tomorrow and pay Charlie a visit. He's more likely to open up to me, and besides, based on what you tell me, it might be a good idea for you to steer clear of Bell City and the Baker boys."

"Thanks, Doc. Bert's giving me a ride to Bell City to pick up my car tomorrow, but I won't linger any longer than necessary."

"Perfect," Doc replied. "Have Bert pick me up on your way and we can go together."

As we approached the boardinghouse, Doc looked up at the sky and observed, "It appears we're in for more bad weather tomorrow."

Inside, Felicity was sitting at the dining room table talking to Leo, who was the last woman left. The table was filled with empty glasses and half-filled bowls of snacks.

Doc gathered up Leo and they said good night.

Felicity and I made small talk for a while. Then she yawned and said, "I'm tired. I think I'll turn in early. Leave the dishes and we'll do them in the morning."

I walked up the stairs with Felicity, hoping that I would get some kind of signal she wanted me to join her. However, when I started to follow her to her room, she turned around, smiled, kissed me on the cheek, and said, "Your room is down that way."

I reluctantly went in the direction she pointed. During the night, I heard intermittent fits of rain on the roof. I hoped that the Kid was keeping dry at Lucky's campsite. I thought about Felicity and hoped that she was thinking about me.

CHAPTER 25

ANOTHER VISIT TO BELL CITY

I came downstairs around a quarter to eight the next morning and walked into the dining room. The mess from last night had been cleaned up. The dining room was empty, so I went into the kitchen. Felicity was at the sink with her back to me, cleaning the last of the previous night's dishes.

"Where is everyone?" I asked.

Felicity turned around and grabbed a dish towel to dry her hands. "Silas left about a half hour ago to drum up some business. Mr. Costello still hasn't returned."

"Maybe he skipped town to avoid paying his bill."

"I doubt it. His bill isn't that much. And besides, most of his belongings are still here. And Fred didn't come home last night," Felicity continued.

"I saw him leave the tavern with Lucky O'Leary last night. I'm a little bit worried about him."

"If he left with Lucky, I'm sure he's okay," Felicity said. "He often goes up in the hills with Lucky to help him mine for gold. He says he prefers working for Lucky more than some of his other jobs. Lucky doesn't talk much, but Fred says it's easier on the ears than working for Mrs. C and Rogers and easier on the feet than working for Indian Charlie. Fred will be back in a day or two. It looks like it's just the two of us for breakfast."

"Sorry," I said, grabbing a banana from the fruit bowl on the kitchen counter. "You're on your own. Bert's picking me up to go get my car, and he should be here just about now. I'll be back in a little while." I peeled the banana, dropped the peel in the garbage, and exited the kitchen, eating as I went.

"Don't let any of those big-time Bell City girls steal your heart away," Felicity hollered after me.

"I'll do my best," I hollered back.

Bert was just pulling up as I walked onto the porch. I went down the steps and climbed in the passenger seat.

"I appreciate the lift," I said to Bert. "Do you mind picking up Doc on the way? He also has business in Bell City."

"No problem," he said. He made a slight detour. Doc was waiting by the curb in front of his house.

It looked like the bad weather was about to return. The sky was filled with dark clouds, and a few raindrops were peppering the windshield.

As we headed out of town, we saw Silas Collins headed down Fourth Street, toting his burlap bag of lightning rods.

"I'm no expert," Bert observed, "but if I were Silas, I don't think I'd want to be walking down the street in the middle of a thunderstorm carrying a bag full of ungrounded metal."

"That does seem risky," I said, "but Silas appears to know his business. He always seems to be able to stay a step or two in front of the lightning."

"Maybe so, but I'd also hate to be two steps away from lightning when it struck."

"You've got a point there, Bert."

Bert explained that he taught second-grade students at the Bell City Elementary School. Although he had a degree in English literature, he preferred teaching younger students.

"Once they reach high school, most kids are set in their ways," Bert said. "You can reach a few of them, but some are already turned off and tuned out. Kids of six and seven are still eager to learn, and it's easier to point them in the right direction."

"Why are you teaching now, in the middle of summer recess?" I asked.

"I teach summer classes and remedial classes and do tutoring at the school for the older students who still care. It's a full-time job these days."

"Does Millie work?" I asked.

"She also teaches second grade in Bell City. Her degree is in ancient history."

"Another class in the same school?"

"No, it's the same class. We split the job; some days I go in and she stays home with the kids. Other days she goes in. We go week by week. We both know the curriculum, so there's no problem with the switch."

"Sort of like Hilda and Frank sharing the diner," I remarked.

"Sort of," Bert laughed, "except there are two of us."

Bert pulled into Harry's garage to drop me off.

"Thanks, Bert," I said, then turning to Doc as I got out, "I'll pick you up when I get done here. Here, you take this." I pulled the bag with the syringe out of my pocket and handed it to Doc. "Maybe Doctor Cooper can do something with it."

Doc nodded. "Charlie's office is at the hospital. I'll wait for you there."

Bert took off for the hospital and I headed in to settle up with Harry. Harry, cigarette still dangling from his mouth, took an arm but thankfully left my leg and gave me the keys to the Buick. I drove her over to the hospital with no problems, pulled into the lot, and waited for Doc.

About fifteen minutes later Doc emerged from the hospital and got in the car.

"Sorry to make you wait. Charlie can get longwinded."

"That's okay. Did you find out anything?"

"Charlie will send the syringe off to the lab to have it tested—without Doctor Baker's knowledge—but he's pretty sure what we're dealing with. Morphine. Billy was taking doses for his pain from the cancer and the treatments."

"How can he be sure?" I asked as I pulled out of the lot.

"He's not sure but Billy was in to see him last week, and Charlie gave him some medication to hold him over and help him get through."

"Wouldn't there be a danger of becoming addicted? And why did he need pain medication?"

"Billy's cancer had returned. Charlie told Billy last week. It had spread throughout his bones. This time there wasn't much chance of a recovery. He didn't tell Billy how much time he had left but he decided there wasn't much danger in giving Billy the morphine. Didn't Annie tell you?" Doc asked, with a confused look on his face.

"She told me the cancer was still in remission. Said Billy was upbeat when he returned from the doctor's office last week."

"I guess Billy didn't tell her," Doc said.

"Or Billy told her, and she didn't want me to know."

I thought maybe it was time to add Annie back to my suspect list.

> CHAPTER 26

ANOTHER VISIT WITH MRS. C

The car drove smoothly on the way back to Cordoba. I dropped Doc off and drove to the boardinghouse.

Felicity was sitting at the dining room table, talking to Sam. The photocopies Sam had taken at the library were laid out on the dining room table in front of Felicity.

"Milo, I was just showing Aunt Felicity our evidence," Sam said.

"I'm afraid it's still not much to go on," I said.

"Well, I've got a plan to see if Mrs. C has the magazines. In one Sherlock Holmes story I read, a woman had blackmail papers hidden in her house. Sherlock disguised himself and visited the woman. While he was in the house, Watson started a fire outside the window. The woman ran to where she had hidden the papers to save them just as Sherlock knew she would do."

"I don't think we should start any fires outside Mrs. C's house. Besides, that Rogers is always keeping an eye on everyone. And it's hard to get in to see Mrs. C. Plus, I left my private detective disguise kit back in San Diego."

"I have a better idea," Felicity jumped in. "Sam, you and Milo go over to Mrs. C's house and tell her you are doing a story about a person you admire for a homework project your father gave you. Tell her you would like to interview her since you have always admired her manners and grace. Mrs. C is a sucker for flattery.

"After you get in, you can keep her occupied while Milo does some snooping."

"We call it investigating, not snooping," I said. "I doubt if that will work, but it's better than starting a fire. What do you say, Sam, want to give it a try?"

"Sure," said Sam.

"You know," said Felicity as she stared at the photo in *Look*, "the features on the woman on the right do resemble a younger Mrs. Cavendish."

I took the page and examined it. "You're right," I said, "which gives me an idea. When I was in her parlor yesterday, I noticed a large painting above the fireplace. The painting appeared to be a picture of her and her husband when they were younger, she was sitting straight-backed in a chair and he was standing beside her with his hand on her shoulder. If you distract her, Sam, I can compare this roller derby picture with the painting of the younger Mrs. C to see if there is any resemblance."

"Right," said Sam, eager to get started, "let's go now."

She headed toward the door and I followed, folding the *Look* page and sticking it in my shirt pocket.

As we got to the door, Felicity called from the dining room, "Take the umbrella. The sky is getting darker."

Sam and I hurried over to Mrs. C's house, sharing the umbrella as the rain was falling harder. We hurried up onto the porch and rang the bell. After several moments, Rogers answered the door, wearing his normal somber expression.

"Yes?" he said.

"We'd like to talk to Mrs. C, if possible," said Sam.

"What is your business?" said Rogers. Before Sam could answer, Mrs. Cavendish, hollered from the parlor, "For heaven's sake, show them in, Rogers. The weather is nasty outside."

Rogers opened the front door and stood aside so we could walk into the hall. As Rogers shut the door behind us, and before he could ask any more questions, Sam ran into the parlor and explained to Mrs. Cavendish about her fictional homework assignment.

"I'll try to help you if I can, but I'm a private person and don't like people snooping into my past," Mrs. C said.

"It's not called snooping, it's investigating," Sam replied.

I thought I saw a slight smile take over the corners of Mrs. C's mouth as she said, "Sit down and we can begin." She motioned to a chair opposite hers. Luckily, Mrs. C's chair was facing away from the fireplace, which was ablaze again, and the painting. I hoped this wouldn't take long, as I was already sweating profusely.

"Of course, you didn't have to bring a bodyguard along, my dear, I assure you I'm harmless," Mrs. C said, motioning toward me.

"Sam just asked me to come along for the company," I said, "and I have to admit that when I was here yesterday, I noticed some of the fine furnishings and antiques in your parlor. Mind if I look around while you talk to Sam?" I could lay on the flattery too.

"All right," Mrs. C said, "but don't go touching everything. Rogers just dusted."

I walked around the room, trying to take in everything while staying as far away from the fire as possible. I pretended to admire several Chinese vases and some reproductions of paintings by the old masters while Sam grilled Mrs. C about her life. As I passed the entrance to the hall on my travels, I noticed a small stand in the parlor just to the right of the door to the hall. The mahogany stand was about three feet tall and measured about two feet on all sides. A vase of flowers was sitting on the top. Beneath was a drawer and underneath the drawer was a compartment with a brass knob and an old-fashioned keyhole with the key in it. I guessed this was where Mrs. C kept her valuables and tried to get a closer look while pretending to smell the flowers. Mrs. C had a clear view of me from her chair, so I decided I couldn't risk looking in the compartment and continued my circuit of the room.

Mrs. C was deep into recollections of her debutante days and the socialite scene in San Francisco when I completed my trip and ended up in front of the fireplace. I nearly tripped over a stack of old newspapers on the floor next to a fireplace stand. The stand held a poker and a long, thin shovel for scooping ashes. I guessed that the newspapers were used by Rogers to start the fire.

I was now standing directly in front of the fire, although I felt like I was entering the gates of Hell. Mrs. Cavendish was seated with her back to me and was engrossed in stories of her pampered upbringing, so I had no problem in getting a closer look at the painting above the fireplace. Sam and I exchanged a quick glance as I pulled the *Look* page out of my pocket and unfolded it.

I glanced down at the photo, then looked up at the painting of the young Mrs. C, ignoring the gentleman standing next to her. I then looked down at the photo, concentrating on the woman on the right. I again looked up at the painting and my eyes widened. Forgetting the situation, I exclaimed, "Well, I'll be…"

At that moment, three things—no, *four* things happened.

First, Mrs. C and Sam both turned to look at me in reaction to my exclamation.

Then, there was a loud crash, like a small explosion on the roof above, followed by a crack of thunder.

Thirdly, the whole house shook from the crash, and an ember jumped from the fireplace near where I was standing and landed on the pile of newspapers, setting them ablaze.

Lastly, Rogers ran in from outside and screamed, "Lightning!"

By now the parlor was filled with smoke, so I acted.

"Rogers, get her out of here," I yelled. "Sam, run for help." I grabbed the poker from the stand and poked at the pile of flaming newspapers.

Sam ran out, but I noticed out of the corner of my eye that Mrs. C took a small detour to the stand near the door. She ignored the compartment with the lock and key but pulled open the drawer above and pulled something out. By this time Rogers was by her side and he said, "Ethel, we have to leave."

Rogers pulled Mrs. C from the house as I continued to fight the fire.

CHAPTER 27

CONFESSIONS

Mrs. Cavendish was now sitting at the dining room table in the boardinghouse, wrapped in a blanket to keep her warm, staring at the copies of *Look* and *TV Guide* in front of her on the dining room table. Also present were Sam, Felicity, Millie, Doc, Leo, and me. Most of the men, other than me and Doc, were over at Mrs. C's house surveying the damage. Doc and Leo had hurried over to check on the condition of Mrs. C. and Rogers, neither of whom seemed worse for the wear. Skipper was out on the lawn in front of the house throwing a ball to Pard, as the weather had cleared up.

"As you can see, and Mr. Forbes already knows, the pictures in these magazines are of me," she said to the group. Then turning to me, "Thank you, Mr. Forbes, for saving my house."

"It was nothing," I said, neglecting to tell her that the fire in the newspapers had dwindled and died of its own accord after she left.

Mrs. Cavendish continued. "I am not who I seem. I grew up poor in Kansas City, near the stockyards on the wrong side of town. As I grew older, I looked for a way out and ended up trying out for the roller derby, which was popular at the time. I could skate some and, if I might say, I was not bad-looking and looked good in the skimpy uniform the girls wore.

"The Kansas City Stars, a professional roller derby team, hired me and gave me the nickname Penny Dreadful—growing up in a tough neighborhood, I was pretty good at throwing an elbow. I began traveling the roller derby circuit. In San Francisco, I met Mr. Cavendish, who was a part owner of the Bay Area Bombers team.

He used to come to the matches and sit in the front row, and he was quite taken with me.

"A romance soon blossomed, and I retired from the derby and we were married and lived in San Francisco. He had inherited a small fortune and lived in San Francisco society, but his wealthy Nob Hill neighbors never accepted a former roller derby queen as part of the group.

"When he died, I got as far away from San Francisco as possible, and Cordoba is as far away from San Francisco as possible. I kept my past a secret to avoid being ostracized again."

"That wouldn't have happened here," said Millie.

"I now know that, my dear," said Mrs. C. "I'm embarrassed for the way I have been acting all these years. And Doc, please forgive me for taking your magazines. I saw my pictures when I was sitting in your waiting room and put them in my pocketbook on an impulse."

"No need to apologize," said Doc.

"I guess you were afraid someone would recognize you and blow your cover," I said.

"Oh, it wasn't that," Rogers jumped in. "There were many valuables in the cabinet by the door she could have taken when the fire started. Jewelry, stocks, cash. But she went right for the magazines.

"When she saw them in Doc's office, she became nostalgic for the old days and wanted to keep them for a moment. Some nights she sits and stares at the photos for a long time, thinking about her past glories," he said tenderly.

"You care a lot about her, don't you," asked Felicity.

"He even forgot himself and called her Ethel when he was getting her out of the house," I chimed in.

Rogers looked at Mrs. C with a confused look on his face, and Mrs. C took his hand and said, "It's all right, dear. The cat's out of the bag now."

She turned to the group and said, "He's my husband, not my butler. Roy was our butler in San Francisco. When I moved here, I brought him with me to keep up pretenses. Over the years our relationship changed, going to first affection and then love. We snuck off to Las Vegas and got married five years ago."

"I guess that means you won't have to keep up the fancy English accent anymore, will you, Roy," I said. "Wait a minute. Your name is Roy?"

"That's right, Milo," he said. "Roy Rogers. My dad was a big fan of the American westerns and named me after the singing cowboy. And the accent is real since I came from the other side."

Mrs. C smiled and said, "So you see, I've gone from being Penny Dreadful to becoming Dale Evans." Then the smile left her face as she took a last glance at the magazines and passed them across the table to Doc. "These belong to you."

Doc opened the copy of *Look* to the last page and stared at the photograph. "You really were quite a looker, weren't you?" He closed the magazine and pushed both the magazines back to Mrs. C. "You keep them. They mean more to you than they do to me."

"But I couldn't," replied Mrs. C. "Your collection…"

"The collection doesn't mean that much. I can do without them."

Leo jumped in. "Will you two stop it before we all start blubbering? You know the magazines mean a great deal to both of you." She gave a nod to Felicity, who got out of her chair and went to the small table under the phone in the hall. She came back with a couple of magazines and laid them on the table.

"I was saving these for your birthday, but I guess I'll have to give them to you early," she said, pointing to copies of the two issues already on the table. "Happy birthday, Doc. Now you both have copies."

"But where did you get them?" asked Doc, surprised.

"I called Fred down in Yuma, and she found them on the Internet. Cost a lot more than the original cover price, I might add." Turning to me, Leo continued, "Fred is my sister, Frederica."

"But why did Felicity have them?" asked Doc.

"I wanted to surprise you, and I was afraid you would go snooping around the house and office."

"Milo says it's called investigating, not snooping," Sam interrupted.

Leo laughed. "When Milo does it, it's called investigating. When Doc and the Flagg sisters do it, it's just plain snooping."

Just then Ben, Phil, and Indian Charlie walked in.

"The damage to the roof and parlor isn't as bad as we expected," Ben said.

"We should be able to fix it up in about a week," Indian Charlie said. "Until then the house is still livable. We temporarily patched the hole in the roof."

"The fire engine came from over in Bell City," Phil said. "They looked around and left since there was nothing for them to do."

"You two are welcome to stay here during the repairs," said Felicity.

"Thank you, dear, and call me Ethel, please," replied Mrs. C, "but after all the excitement, I think I would like to get home and relax." She and Roy rose from the table to leave.

"Again, thank you all for everything."

"You're welcome, Mrs. Cavendish—I mean Ethel—and maybe you and Roy can join us for the next movie night," Felicity said.

"We'd love to," Ethel replied.

"I'll reserve you a seat."

"You'll do nothing of the sort," complained Mrs. C. "We'll sit wherever is available, same as everybody else."

"Maybe Phil can get hold of an old western for you, Roy."

"Mighty kindly of you, missy," Roy said with a decent John Wayne imitation. "And I'd advise everyone to avoid the seat next to Ethel. Sometimes she forgets where she is, and she's still good with the elbows."

The last remark earned Roy an elbow as they walked onto the porch.

Sam ran after them. "And maybe you can teach me how to roller skate," she exclaimed.

Mrs. C. turned. "Well, at my age I'm afraid my knees won't let me lace on the skates, but I'd be glad to give you some pointers. Stop by sometime and I'll show you some of my old mementos. They've been hidden away in the attic for many years."

"I'll be over tomorrow morning," Sam yelled, and Ethel and Roy walked down the street to their home, hand in hand.

CHAPTER 28

MR. CHURCH

D eciding I should think about the events of the last few days, I took a walk myself. I determined that the best place to be alone in Cordoba was the Municipal Building, so I headed over to my office.

As expected, the building was empty when I got there, so I settled into my chair, put my feet up on the desk, and reviewed the past few days. Aside from a tragic death that may or may not have been a homicide, a mysterious stranger lurking around a diner that was owned and operated by two people who were actually the same person, and the case of the missing magazines, my stay had so far been uneventful.

At least the magazine fiasco has been sorted out, I thought, though the successful conclusion was more from the efforts of a nine-year-old girl than anything I had done. I consoled myself with the fact that I had bigger fish to fry.

Back to Billy Webster. Was it an accident? Murder? Maybe suicide. Chief Baker and Jim Turner held grudges against Bill, and both had access to the plane and parachute. Motive and opportunity. Why did Annie Webster lie about Billy's condition? Or didn't he tell her?

And what about Costello? Why was he so interested in Frank's diner? Maybe the two cases were related.

By this time, I was confusing myself. "Slow down and take it one step at a time," I said to myself out loud. "You've got all afternoon, and no one will disturb you here."

Just then a face appeared in the open door to the office, followed by a small, thin body. "Am I interrupting something?" the face said, peering at me through thick glasses and looking around for whoever I was talking to.

"No, just talking to myself," I said. "Come on in."

The small, thin man with thick glasses and a stylish comb-over walked in. He had a squeaky voice to match his mousy appearance.

"Are you the sheriff?" he asked as he approached the desk.

"If I'm not, I better get my feet off his desk before he returns," I said with a straight face, and then added, "You're not the sheriff, are you?"

"No, no," he responded, and then realizing I was kidding, laughed a squeaky laugh, and still unsure said, "You are the sheriff, aren't you?"

"Yes, I am," I responded honestly this time, removing my feet from the top of the desk. "Come in and sit down. What can I do for you?"

The man sat down, reached in his pocket for his wallet, pulled out a business card, and placed it on the desk so I could read it, although there was no need since he introduced himself.

"My name is Church, and I work for the Arrowhead Insurance Company." He reached over and shook my hand.

Before he could continue, I interrupted. "Sorry, Mr. Church, but I'm not interested in purchasing any insurance. A man in my position is unlikely to get into risky situations, and I can carry a gun in case I do."

"Oh, I'm not selling insurance. I'm an investigator with Arrowhead, and I'm looking into the death of William Webster, who had an insurance policy with us. You see, you and I are in similar lines of business."

After I had stopped shuddering from the last remark, I asked Church, "Why come and see me?"

"I heard you were investigating the tragic accident."

"Yes, that's true."

"Was there any indication that maybe this wasn't an accident?" Church asked.

"I have nothing conclusive to dispel the notion it wasn't an accident," I said, trying not to emphasize the word *conclusive*. I was trying to walk a thin line between telling Church what I discovered and keeping my suspicions close to the vest. "Why do you ask?"

"This is standard procedure on large payouts."

"I'm confused," I responded. "I was led to believe that Billy's policy was only ten thousand dollars. That doesn't seem like a large payout."

"That's true, but there was an accidental death clause that pays ten times the face value if the death is a result of an accident."

"So Arrowhead is on the hook for a hundred grand?"

"Yes, unless his death wasn't an accident. And don't get the wrong impression. Arrowhead's business is insurance. We don't consider ourselves 'on the hook,' as you say. We'll pay the money once the investigation is completed."

"Do you have any reason to believe that Billy's death was anything other than an accident?" I asked.

"Quite the contrary," said Church. "Everything seems to indicate an accident, and the cause of death is listed as accidental on the death certificate."

Dr. Baker doesn't waste time, I thought.

"And we're prepared to pay the hundred thousand to Mrs. Webster. I wanted to check with you to cover all the bases."

"I have no conclusive evidence to prove that it was other than an accident."

"Well, if you should find something conclusive," he said, emphasizing the word *conclusive*, "please call me. My number is on the card."

With that Church got up, gave me a slight smile, and started walking out of the office.

"Mr. Church," I called before he got to the door.

"Yes," he said, turning around.

"What if Billy committed suicide? Would the company refuse to pay?"

"The policy also has a suicide clause that states no payment will be made if the insured commits suicide within a year of purchasing the policy. Since Mr. Webster's policy was taken out more than a year ago, Arrowhead is still obligated to make payment. However, if Mr. Webster committed suicide, the payout would be ten thousand rather than one hundred thousand, since the death would not be considered accidental."

Mr. Church turned and left, leaving me to ponder the situation again. The coroner had already ruled the death accidental, so I could justifiably conclude my investigation. But what was Dr. Baker's rush in issuing the death certificate? And what about the harness and the syringe and Billy's enemies? There were more loose ends than a nearsighted spinster's afghan.

I looked for something to take my mind off the problem for a while, but the only distraction I could find in the office was the Archie comic book Ben had used to swear me in. I picked it up and absentmindedly started leafing through the pages.

As usual, the main plot involved Archie stealing Veronica away from Reggie as he has been doing for the last fifty or sixty years. The last frame showed Archie and Veronica walking away and Reggie standing there with steam coming out of his ears.

That's when I decided to pay a visit to Jim Turner.

CHAPTER 29

JIM TURNER

T he ride to Chiquita was about the same as every other ride I had taken in this area, dusty and monotonous. I drove the same route we had taken to the fair. Chiquita was a few miles past the fairgrounds. It was another small town with some businesses on the main street and a few side streets.

I hadn't asked for directions to the sheriff's office before I left, figuring I'd have no trouble finding the place, and I was right. I pulled into the small lot next to the police station and found my way to Jim Turner's desk.

The Chiquita sheriff's office was an open area with three desks, two in the front on opposite walls and facing each other, and one in the back of the room, Jim's desk, facing toward the entrance. Jim was talking to a man I assumed was a deputy at the desk on the right. The left-hand desk was occupied by a woman, maybe a deputy, maybe a secretary.

Jim was wearing a white short-sleeve shirt and jeans and cowboy boots.

I walked over and introduced myself.

"I remember you from the other day," Jim said. "What can I do for you?" Jim didn't seem thrilled to see me.

"I want to touch base with you on the Billy Webster death," I said.

"I thought the investigation was done. Didn't the coroner rule accidental death?"

"Yes, but I want to tie up a few loose ends. I understand you grew up with Billy."

"Let's take a walk," Jim said, grabbing a cowboy hat off a hook in the wall and ushering me out of the building. It was obvious he didn't want to talk in front of the others in the room.

We walked down the street past a Laundromat and a bowling alley called the Chiquita Lanes, which, judging by its width, held about three alleys. Next to the bowling alley was a dive called the Red Parrot. Jim grabbed the door and walked in, with me following behind. I stood a moment and waited for my eyes to adjust from the bright sunlight to the darkness of the bar but realized no period of adjustment would allow me to see beyond five feet since there was little lighting inside.

This didn't matter as there was little to see. The Red Parrot had a bar running the length of the room on the left wall; on the right wall, there were four or five small round tables with two cane-backed chairs at each table. That was it, except for a door between two of the tables on the right-hand wall that I assumed connected with the bowling alley.

No television, no pool table, no music. Just the bar, some barstools, tables and chairs, and the barstools and chairs were all empty. The only person in the bar besides me and Jim—unless someone was sitting in the back of the bar beyond my scope of vision—was the bartender, a grizzled old man who hadn't shaved in about a week. I hoped that he had bathed during that time.

Jim, who hadn't spoken since we left his office, walked up to the bar and ordered a beer; then he turned and looked at me, still without speaking.

"The same," I said.

The bartender grabbed two kitchen glasses, held them up to the only light in the room, a ceiling fixture with a bare bulb of about sixty watts, and wiped one of the glasses with a bar rag which was flung across his shoulder. He then filled the glasses and placed them on the bar. Jim threw two quarters on the bar, which I assumed was enough to cover both beers. The bartender took the money, tossed it on the counter behind the bar, and went through a door at the back of the building. During the whole exchange, he had not spoken a word. I didn't know where he was going, but I was hoping for a bath or even a shave.

Jim grabbed one beer and headed a table, saying, "Let's sit at a table where we can have some privacy."

After the scene I described, I leave it to you to determine how incongruous that statement was.

I grabbed the other beer and took a quick look at the glass while I still had the benefit of the lightbulb. Fortunately, the glass did not look substantially dirtier than those found in my kitchen, but not nearly as clean as the ones found in Felicity's.

After we were seated, I attempted to break the ice.

"Should you be drinking on duty?" I asked.

"It's almost quitting time," Jim responded, "and should you be drinking on duty, Sheriff?"

I will point out at this point that there will be a lack of descriptions of Jim's facial expressions, since I could not see Jim's face, which was at least three feet away from mine.

Having forgotten that I was also a sheriff, I continued.

"What can you tell me about Billy?" I asked.

"Not much," Jim responded. "We grew up together and were friends then but haven't been close for a long time. I'm sure you heard the story from others." By the tone of his voice, I pictured a wry smile.

"Annie Lee?"

"As I said, I'm sure you heard the story already."

"Do you still have feelings for her?"

"I have feelings for everyone I know, some good, some bad. I thought you wanted to talk about Billy."

"I hear you two were always interested in flying. Was Billy careful about jumping?"

"As far as I know. We did some jumping in high school, and he was always careful to inspect his gear. Why? Was something wrong with his chute?"

I didn't answer but continued with my questions. "You spend time at the airport, don't you?"

"I fly the plane occasionally."

"The day before the accident?"

"Yes, I was there." Jim was becoming agitated. "And yes, I had access to the parachute. But I had no reason to kill Billy. My thing with Annie was long in the past, and if I still had a beef with Billy, I would have faced him like a man. Why don't you go talk to Chief Baker if you want to talk to someone who had a grudge against Billy?"

"I already had an encounter with the chief," I said. I waited a minute without speaking, giving Jim a chance to settle down and to see if he had anything else to say.

Finally, he said more calmly, "Do you have reason to suspect that Billy's death was more than an accident?"

"I'm just doing my job," I said.

"Look, Billy and I were no longer close, but we were best friends in high school and you don't forget those things. I wouldn't do anything to hurt either him or Annie. And this was only a tragic accident. Why don't you leave it alone and let Billy rest in peace?"

"I will when I'm satisfied that I've done what I can," I answered.

I got up and walked out the door, leaving Jim sitting at the table.

CHAPTER 30

THE CRIME SCENE

I t was mid-afternoon when I drove out of Chiquita. The fair was again in full swing when I drove past, and I thought of stopping for a bite to eat but decided against it as I had other things on my mind. Everyone I talked to seemed to want me to stop looking into Billy's death. Jim Turner seemed to be a more likable guy than Chief Baker, but he was no more cooperative.

As I came to the intersection with County Line Road, I decided that maybe it was a good idea to check out the crime scene again. I hadn't had a good look at it the day Billy fell, with everyone crowding around, and I didn't think I would find much after all the traffic got through with it, but it seemed like something a sheriff ought to do.

I pulled over to the side of the road and walked over to the area where Billy had landed. The rain of the previous day had soaked the area, which was now drying out in the desert sun, so the ground was hardening again. There were remnants of the many footprints that had littered the area, but not much else as I walked around. On closer inspection, there seemed to be an indentation in the ground a little way from the area where Billy landed, but the combination of tracks from the crowd and the rain made the marks, if there were any, indistinguishable.

The surrounding area was flat land in all directions, apart from the intersecting roads and a few cactus and bushes scattered about. Seeing nothing of interest, I was ready to leave but decided to walk around the perimeter of the area. I walked around in ever-increasing circles, trying to cover most of the ground around the accident site.

Finding nothing of interest, I was heading back to my car when the glint of a shiny object caught my eye from the middle of some low bushes a good distance away from the intersection. I went over to investigate.

CHAPTER 31

A TALK WITH BEN

T he rest of the drive back to Cordoba was spent trying to clear my mind and determine my next steps. I decided to have a talk with Ben Nye. I was hoping to catch him in his office, rather than at the diner, so I could speak to him privately. I found him at his desk.

He was reading a newspaper, a portion of which was lying on his desk. As I entered and sat down, I saw that the banner on the paper read "Bell City Bugle".

Ben greeted me, then tapped the paper with his finger and said, "Billy Webster's funeral is today. The paper said the coroner ruled his death an accident, so I guess your sheriff duties are over."

"Pretty soon. I already know the coroner's verdict," I told Ben, recapping my visit from Mr. Church.

"Let me ask you a question," I continued. "Ethically speaking, do you think it's immoral to keep your mouth shut if you may know information which may or may not be definitive, but if you reveal it, it might negatively affect the lives of others?"

"I'm no expert on ethics," Ben said. "If you're talking about something like telling your wife that a dress makes her look fat, keeping quiet may be the wisest decision on a number of fronts. But I get the impression that your question is not rhetorical and that we're speaking of more serious matters."

"Yes," I responded. "If there is something that is just speculation and I can't prove it, but I'm pretty sure it may be accurate, my obligations are a little fuzzy."

"Sounds like you're walking a fine line between speculation and gossip," Ben said.

"More than gossip," I replied. "I took a trip out to Chiquita today, and on the way back, I stopped..."

"Hold it right there," Ben interrupted me. "I think you better not reveal too much. I am an elected official, and I also have a reputation around town, mostly earned, of disseminating information a little too freely.

"As I said, I'm a little weak on ethical rules, but it seems to me that a good man generally makes good decisions and a bad man will make bad decisions. Not always, but as long as a good man can sleep well at night, I would trust his judgment.

"But I want to remind you, you are also an appointed officer. Although the ceremony was not too dignified, you swore to uphold the laws of the State of California, and I would expect you to do that."

"Got it," I said, sure of what I would do, "and I don't think I'll be needing this any longer." I pulled the wallet with the badge from my pocket and placed it on Ben's desk. "I've done what I could and will be heading back to San Diego in the next day or so."

"I accept your resignation," Ben said with a slight smile. "I appreciate your helping me out."

Ben returned the wallet to his desk drawer and I got up to leave. As I walked out the door, Ben said, "You're a good man, Milo."

CHAPTER 32

ANOTHER TALK WITH DR. BAKER

I was still unclear how to proceed, but I knew what the next step was. I drove to Bell City and pulled into the hospital parking lot.

It was late afternoon and most of the action was going the other way, employees leaving for home. I took the elevator to the third floor and headed for the medical examiner's office.

The secretary looked up when she saw me enter, then went back to what she was doing.

I walked up and said, "I'd like to speak to Dr. Baker."

"He's just leaving. You'll have to wait until tomorrow," she responded.

"This won't take long," I said as I walked past her to Dr. Baker's office door. The secretary offered only token resistance, and I got the feeling she didn't care.

Just as I reached the office, the door opened and Dr. Baker appeared in the doorway, his suit jacket halfway on as he prepared to leave.

"I'd like to talk to you a minute," I said.

"It'll have to wait. I'm leaving for the day," he responded.

"It can't wait," I said.

"If you don't leave, I'll…"

"You'll what, call the police? I'm sure you have the number on speed dial. Go ahead. Maybe your brother should hear what I have to say."

Dr. Baker finished putting on his jacket, walked a few steps back into his office, and said, "Make it quick."

"Aren't you going to offer me a seat?"

"No, you're not going to be here that long. Now tell me what you want, or I will call the police."

I got right down to the point of my visit.

"I have certain doubts about the cause of Billy Webster's death. What are my chances of getting you to reopen the coroner's investigation?"

"Slim and none," replied Dr. Baker, "and Slim just left the building. Now if that's all you came here for, I'll be on my way."

"But what if I told you I discovered some new evidence and have a theory..."

"Do you have proof that the death wasn't an accident?"

"Well, no, but..."

"Then the official cause remains accidental death. Billy Webster is dead and buried, and I'm not going to spend any more time on this. I would advise you to complete your investigation also. Now if you don't mind, I'm late for dinner."

"Maybe you're right, Doc," I said as he brushed past me and headed out of the building. I had gotten the response I expected, and I was satisfied with that response. Still, a fellow has to try.

I was right behind Dr. Baker as he headed to his car, and I decided to follow him. I pulled out right behind him and stayed a few car lengths behind. He turned onto Main Street, drove a few blocks, and as I expected, pulled into the parking lot of the Bell City Police Department. I doubted that he had a dinner date with Chief Baker.

I drove past the station and headed out of town toward Shady Acres. Somehow, I had a feeling that I might have a police escort on my trip back through Bell City on my way home.

This was fine with me. As I said, I've never been punched in the face. I've also never punched a police chief in the face. I reckoned that Bell City was as good a place as any to cross both those activities off my bucket list.

CHAPTER 33

ANOTHER TALK WITH ANNIE WEBSTER

A s I drove up to the trailer park, I looked at the cemetery across the street, I wondered how many residents of Shady Acres Trailer Park had changed their addresses to Shady Acres Cemetery over the years as Billy had, assuming he had been buried there.

I was hoping to find Annie at home alone, but when I pulled up in front of her trailer, her driveway was full of cars, and there were several more parked out front.

I drove past the trailer and found a spot to park, then walked back to the trailer. The front door was open. Through the screen door, I heard several conversations going on. I walked in and found the front room full of people, mourners who had come over to Annie's after the funeral.

There were about a dozen men and women, none of whom I recognized except Turkey Trotz. He was trying to resurrect the seventies, wearing a lime-green polyester leisure suit, pink shirt, and purple tie. Standing among a group of men in black suits and white shirts, he stood out like a peacock at a penguin convention.

Most of the women were on the other side of the room talking. I didn't see Annie among them. On the table in the middle was a buffet with several casseroles and plates of appetizers I assumed were provided by the guests. On a corner table were several bottles of liquor and soft drinks and an ice bucket.

As I surveyed the scene, Annie walked in from the kitchen, holding a platter of little meatballs with toothpicks through them. She saw me and placed the platter on the table and walked over.

"Thanks for coming," she said. "Would you like anything to eat or drink?"

Although I hadn't eaten much all day, I wasn't hungry. But I had a feeling I could use a little drink before having my conversation with Annie.

"Nothing to eat, but I'll take a drink."

Annie led me across the room in a crisscross pattern to avoid the crowd of people that exceeded the maximum capacity of the trailer. I grabbed a meatball on the way across as we headed for the table that held the drinks.

"There's beer in the refrigerator if you'd prefer," Annie offered.

"No thanks, this is fine," I said, locating a bottle of bourbon and filling a glass halfway, then adding ice. "How are you holding up?"

"All right so far. I assume it will get harder after all the people leave."

After taking a good-sized swallow, I said, "Is there somewhere we can talk?"

Annie looked around at the crowd, then grabbed my elbow and said, "Come with me."

She led me through the kitchen and out the back door to a couple of plastic chairs surrounding a plastic table located under the kitchen window.

"Won't you be missed inside?" I asked.

"I'm the last person everyone wants to talk to. Everyone comes over to offer their condolences, but after that the conversation gets awkward and nobody knows what to say, including me, so everyone drifts off to join their little groups."

"I guess that's human nature," I said. "Listen, I want to talk to you about Billy's death. Is that okay?"

"Yes, I want to get all of this behind me as quickly as possible and get on with mine and Billy Jr.'s lives. But what do you want to talk about? It was an accident, wasn't it? That's what the death certificate says."

"I'm not so sure. After his visit to the doctor last week, did Billy tell you his cancer was back?"

Annie looked at me with an expression of shock on her face. "No, he told me the cancer was still in remission and everything was fine."

"I'm afraid that was not the case. Dr. Cooper told him the cancer had returned and that it had progressed to the point where it was untreatable. Had Billy shown any recent signs of regression?"

"He'd lost weight and complained of some aches and pains, but he said it wasn't serious. I don't understand. He was in a good mood when he returned from the doctor, and he was happier in the last week than he's been in a long time."

"He didn't want you to know."

"But why?"

"I don't think Billy's death was accidental," I said. I explained about the parachute that appeared to have been tampered with and the syringe that was found on the plane.

"Do you think someone cut Billy's parachute so he would fall?" she asked.

"Yes. Do you recognize this?" I pulled a small pocketknife with a pearl handle from my pocket.

"That's Billy's knife."

"I found this in the bushes a short distance from where he fell. And there were marks on the ground indicating that's where Billy planned on landing."

"But what does it all mean?" Annie asked, confused.

"I think Billy committed suicide. He planned this out to look like an accident. I think he cut his parachute partway through so the parachute would stay together during his jump. He cut it under the buckle, thinking no one would notice.

"Then sometime while he was in the plane, or maybe before, he shot himself up with the morphine he got from Dr. Cooper."

"Would he have taken enough to kill him?"

"I don't know. Maybe he had been saving it up so he would have a lethal dose. Dr. Cooper sent the syringe for tests, but I don't think there's any way of telling how much he took. I think he took enough to the point where he wouldn't be feeling any pain or be too conscious, but conscious enough to do what he had to do.

"Then he jumped, and when he got to the right altitude and had steered his parachute to the right spot, he cut the chute through with his knife—this would have been easy since the leather was cut through most of the way beforehand—and let it fall away. He threw the knife as far away as possible, hoping it wouldn't be found. He had already picked out a spot to aim for beforehand."

"But why pick that spot?" Annie asked.

"I think maybe he picked the spot across the County Line Road so he wouldn't end up in Jim Turner's county. Maybe he didn't want Jim to dig into his death. He would have known if he landed in Cordoba's jurisdiction, there would be less of an investigation. Unfortunately, Ben Nye got me involved.

"But I'm not sure Billy had planned it that way. He probably just picked a spot far enough from the fairground so you wouldn't see him hit."

"But why make it look like an accident? Didn't he want me to know?"

"I'm sure he didn't want you to know, but there was also the insurance policy."

Annie turned angry. "Don't tell me that Billy killed himself for a ten-thousand-dollar insurance policy!"

"No. It was mostly the cancer. Dr. Parker told Billy he didn't have long, and with the pain, the rest of the time wasn't going to be pleasant. But there was also an accidental death clause in Billy's insurance policy, so that if he died by accident, you would receive a hundred thousand rather than ten thousand dollars."

Annie's expression turned to one of surprise. "I didn't know," she said. I was sure she didn't. "What happens next?"

"Well, I talked to Dr. Baker, and he's not inclined to change the death certificate, so Billy's official cause of death is accidental. That may help later with explaining the death to Billy Jr."

Annie shook her head. "No, when he gets old enough, he'll know the truth. I wouldn't want to live with the lie."

I nodded. "As far as the insurance goes, the death certificate says it was accidental. That seems to be good enough for the insurance company. An investigator named Church came to visit me earlier today, and he seemed inclined to close the case since there was nothing indicating anything other than an accidental death."

"I got a call from Mr. Church today. He's coming to see me tomorrow. Why won't Dr. Baker consider reopening the case?"

"I don't know. Both he and Chief Baker have been antagonistic. Dr. Baker knows there was a feud between the chief and Billy. Then I show up and tell him Billy's death may not have been an accident. Maybe he's trying to protect his brother.

"As far as Chief Baker, he just doesn't want someone he doesn't have under his thumb looking into the investigation. He wants to run me out of town just on principle."

"Did you tell Mr. Church your suspicions?"

"No. At that point, I hadn't yet found the knife. And besides, that's all they are, suspicions. The chute was old and could have already been torn. If he took the morphine, maybe he wanted to alleviate the pain. Who knows why the knife was there? Maybe Billy got tangled up in the chute when it ripped, and he tried to cut himself free with the knife."

"What do you think I should tell Mr. Church?"

"That's up to you. Even if you mention my suspicions, he can't prove the death wasn't accidental." Then I added, "A wise man once told me that good people generally make good decisions, so I'm not worried about you." I looked out over the empty terrain to the horizon far away and pointed. "A hundred thousand dollars would be enough to find out what's on the other side of this desert."

"At this point, I'm not so sure I want to know. It could be just like this on a larger scale, or worse. At least here, there's a roomful of people in there who cared about Billy and who care about me and Billy Jr. Who knows what I would find out there?"

"Well, I've told you what I know," I said, standing up to leave. "I'll be heading back there myself soon." I pointed across the desert again. I didn't tell her that her opinion of the outside world wasn't far off.

"Can you see yourself out?" Annie asked. "I want to sit here a while longer and think."

"Sure," I responded, "and I'm sorry I had to tell you this."

"Don't be. At least I know that Billy died happy."

"What do you mean?"

"Didn't you see the way he spread his arms when he was falling? And I bet there was a smile on his face.

"He finally got to fly like an eagle."

CHAPTER 34

THE BEGINNING OF THE END

I made it out of Bell City without incident, which is for the best.

I slept well that night. The temperature in the desert drops rapidly at night. While the days in Cordoba were hot and oppressive, the evenings were pleasant and even cool, and I used several blankets at night since I slept with the window open.

When I went downstairs the next morning, Costello was sitting at the dining room table waiting for breakfast. I went into the kitchen, where Felicity was preparing pancakes, and learned that Costello returned late the previous night but that the Kid had not yet returned, and that Silas had gone over to Mrs. C's to make a sale, at her request this time.

I grabbed a cup of coffee and returned to the dining room. I thought it was about time I found out what Costello was up to. After a little small talk, during which I learned that he had gone to Vegas for a few days (or so he said) to relieve the monotony, I said to Costello, "If you don't mind, I'd like to sit down with you after breakfast and find out a little more about why you came to Cordoba."

"Certainly, Milo, I have no objections. And I've been meaning to have a talk with you about some of your actions." He had a sinister smile on his face, which Felicity and I both noticed as she was bringing a platter of pancakes into the room.

She set down the platter next to a pitcher of hot maple syrup. There was also butter and a jar of jam, along with pitchers of milk and orange juice and a carafe of coffee.

"But for now," Costello continued, "let's enjoy Felicity's wonderful cooking."

I agreed and Felicity sat down and all three of us dug in.

About halfway through, the front door opened and the Kid walked in, looking dusty and tired. He was followed a minute later by Lucky O'Leary. By the looks of the dirt and dust that covered them, I guessed that the desert floor east of here was at least an inch lower.

"Come in and get something to eat, Fred," Felicity addressed the Kid.

"Thanks," replied the Kid, "but I better get cleaned up first. I don't want to dirty up your dining room."

"Nonsense," replied Felicity, "the pancakes will get cold. Besides, this is my cleaning day anyway." She dragged the Kid into the dining room and turned to Lucky, who was standing expectantly near the front door.

"You come too, Lucky," Felicity said. "There's plenty for everyone."

"Much obliged," said Lucky. "I could do with a bite and a cup of java."

Felicity grabbed plates, utensils, and napkins from the sideboard along the wall and set places for the Kid and Lucky. She grabbed a cup, poured Lucky a coffee and moved the cream and sugar within his reach. He avoided the cream but added enough spoonsful of sugar to raise the coffee level in the cup about a half inch.

"Have you been out to Lucky's claim, helping him mine for gold?" Felicity asked the Kid as she reseated herself.

"Yes, but all I found was rain and dust and little critters crawling around."

"And a dead body," said Lucky nonchalantly, tucking a napkin into the top of his shirt.

I noticed Costello straighten up, stop eating, and stare at Lucky. "You found a dead body out in the desert?" he asked.

"Well, it wasn't a whole body, just a bunch of bones. Picked clean. Looked like they had been out there quite a while."

"Do you remember where you found the bones?" asked Costello.

"I reckon I could find them again. With all the rain we had, it's easy to follow the tire tracks."

"Could you take me out there?"

"Well, I'll be going out to my claim after breakfast, and where we found the body is on the way. But you'll have to take your own car so I don't have to drive all the way back to town and drop you off."

"It's a deal," said Costello.

After breakfast, the Kid went upstairs for a bath, and Felicity cleaned up. Lucky got up, stretched, and headed for his jeep.

Costello also rose. "I'm afraid our little talk will have to wait until we return," he said.

"We?" I asked.

"Of course. You are coming with me, aren't you?" Again, the sinister smile.

"Sure," I said. "I haven't seen a skeleton since high school biology class."

As we got up to leave, Felicity said, "Milo, could you help in the kitchen for a minute?" I followed her into the kitchen while Costello headed for the porch.

Once we were in the kitchen and out of hearing range, Felicity said, "I don't think you should go with him. He scares me. And you remember what Skipper said about the gun."

"Don't worry," I said. "I'll be okay. He's probably just an anatomist studying skeletal remains."

"Yes, but he's an anatomist who is packing heat. Is that the way you say it?"

"Well, I've never said it quite like that, but I get the idea. Don't worry, I'll be fine."

"Okay but be careful."

I headed out to the porch, where Costello was waiting. Lucky was revving the engine of his jeep, waiting for us.

"We'll take your car," said Costello. "The trunk of the compact car from the rental agency isn't big enough to hold a body." I hoped he was joking.

I wasn't sure if he was referring to the body of a skeleton or one with more flesh on it, like mine, but I was sure he wouldn't try anything since too many people knew we were together. I was more worried about what the bumps and grinds of the desert roads would do to my new axle.

Lucky took the road out of town heading east. Costello and I did little talking. We both realized that the time for talking would come after we had seen the body and returned.

When we came to a crossroads, Lucky turned right onto County Line Road, rather than continue toward Chiquita. I did the same. The road became harder to follow and eventually disappeared. After another fifteen minutes, Lucky veered to his left, heading toward some foothills a little way off in the distance. We could see the tire tracks made previously in the rain, now hardened. Another ten minutes and the jeep pulled up by the side of a hill that rose for about twenty feet and then flattened out at the top.

Lucky got out of the jeep, and Costello and I followed. The skeleton he had mentioned was lying in a heap at the bottom of the hill. It wasn't really a skeleton but rather a pile of bones, clearly human, scattered around the immediate area. It looked like a complete set, but then I wasn't counting.

Costello walked over and stooped down to get a closer look. I decided I was close enough where I was.

"Interesting," he said as he stared at the bones. Turning to look at Lucky, he asked, "Do you have a shovel with you?"

"Got one in the back of the jeep." Lucky ambled off to fetch it.

When he returned, Costello said, "I think I'll take a little look at the top of this hill." He took the shovel and started climbing. The hill was not steep, but Costello, not in the best physical condition and carrying a shovel, had a hard time negotiating the climb. When he reached the plateau on top, he walked around for a short time, occasionally scraping the ground with the shovel, not really digging.

I stayed at the bottom of the hill with Lucky, thinking the chances were slim that Costello would find another body. Also, I was hot and not the finest physical specimen myself, so I wanted to avoid the climb up the hill.

As Lucky and I were staring at the bones, he said, "Some hiker or prospector who got lost in the desert and died of thirst. The body has been here quite a spell, and the vultures have picked the bones clean."

Overhearing this, Costello hollered down, "And mighty tidy vultures they were, since they also took the trouble to bury his clothes up here."

Hearing this, I realized I couldn't further avoid climbing the hill, so I scrambled up, followed from behind by Lucky.

We saw when we reached the top that Costello had uncovered a pile of old clothing buried about a foot under the dirt. What I call clothing was rather a pile of scraps of mildewed material lying in a heap in the hole. On closer inspection, I could make out a battered pair of shoes and something that may have at one time been a belt among the scraps. An old potato sack was lying next to the clothes.

"What do you make of it?" I asked Costello, who was now bent over, examining the pile.

"I have my theories, but that will have to wait." He reached down and removed something from the pile, then stood up and held out his open hand toward me. "What do you make this is?"

He held a small round object in his hand. It was made of metal, was gold in color, and had a small insignia like a coat of arms imprinted on the front. Costello turned it over; it had a small loop on the back.

"Looks like a button of some sort, the kind you would find on a suit jacket or blazer, presumably worn by the fellow at the bottom of the hill." For some reason, I thought if Sam were here, she would chastise me for assuming the skeleton was male. I hadn't inspected it close enough to determine the sex, and even if I had, I wouldn't know what to look for.

Costello was not interested in my detective skills, or lack thereof. He reached into his pocket. For a moment I thought of Felicity's warning, but he withdrew his hand and showed me a button, identical to the one he had just found in the hole.

Confused, I said, "But where...?"

Before I could finish, Costello said, "I found this button in the old tank behind the diner the night you followed me."

"But what does it all mean?" I asked.

"Again, I have my theories," Costello replied, "but I'd rather not discuss them until we get back to town and I can clean up a little and get a cold drink."

He then became silent and stared down at the pile of clothing with a quizzical look, as if undecided what he should do next. After staring at the pile for about a minute, he turned his back to us and walked a distance away and stared out into the desert. I heard him softy whistling another classical music tune I couldn't identify. This one sounded like a waltz.

Lucky and I stood and stared at Costello's back without talking. Five minutes later, he snapped his fingers, stopped whistling, and turned and walked back to where we were standing.

He gathered up the articles in the hole, stuffed them in the potato sack, and refilled the hole. "C'mon," he said as he clumsily descended the hill, carrying the sack.

When we all had reached the bottom, Costello turned to Lucky. "I'd like you to do me a favor if you don't mind."

"Depends on what you're askin'," replied Lucky.

"I want you to take this sack back to your campsite and burn it and everything inside. Can you do that for me?"

"I reckon I can, if that's what you want."

"That's what I want."

Costello handed the sack to Lucky, who threw it in the back of his jeep, climbed in, and drove off further into the desert. He seemed to be unfazed by the preceding events.

Costello took one more look at the pile of bones and headed to my car.

"Are we going to take them back with us?" I asked, gesturing toward the bones.

"We'll leave them here," he said. "Better not tamper with the evidence any more than we already have."

"You're beginning to sound like a cop," I said.

"Well, what do you think I am, a Mafia hitman or something? A sharp fellow like you must have figured that out already." Again, he gave me a sinister grin.

"Who do you work for? The FBI? CIA?"

"Those are just initials. Let's say I'm on Uncle Sam's payroll."

We got in the car and I turned to head back to town. Costello did not speak on the drive back. I had a lot of questions, but it was clear I wouldn't get any answers until we were back in Cordoba.

I wasn't confident I would get many answers there, either.

CHAPTER 35

MORE INTRIGUE AT THE DINING ROOM TABLE

F elicity was sitting on the porch, reading, when we returned. Our disheveled appearance made us look a lot
like Lucky O'Leary without the hat.

"What have you two been up to?" she asked with slight alarm.

"First a cleanup, then the questions," Costello replied as he
walked up the dining room stairs. I gave Felicity a dumbfounded
look but said nothing and followed Costello upstairs.

We took turns washing up and changing our clothes and returned to the dining room together. Felicity was sitting there
waiting for us.

"Can I get you something to drink?" she asked us. "You must
be thirsty. How about a glass of iced tea?"

"Have you got anything stronger?" Costello asked.

"Well, I keep some wine around. Other than that, there's not
much." Suddenly remembering, she said, "I have an unopened
bottle of bourbon somewhere that a salesman who stayed here left
me a year or two ago. He said after a week in Cordoba, mingling
with the local citizens, he had decided to quit drinking and check
into a clinic."

"That will do nicely," Costello said. "I'd like a glass of tea with a
shot of bourbon in it."

"I'll have the same," I said, "but hold the tea." After the events
of the day and anticipating Costello's explanation, I needed something to settle my nerves.

Felicity went into the kitchen to get the drinks. We could hear
her wandering around, opening and shutting cabinet doors,
searching for the bottle of bourbon.

A short time later she returned with a tray holding a bottle of Old Grand-Dad, a pitcher of iced tea, a bottle of ginger ale, and three tall glasses filled with ice cubes.

"I thought you might prefer ginger ale to tea with your bourbon," she said.

She set the tray down and poured herself a ginger ale. Costello grabbed the bottle of bourbon, opened it, and filled his glass about halfway. He then filled the glass with ginger ale and took a sip. I poured a lot of bourbon and a little ginger ale and ice in my glass, and Felicity and I both took a big slug of our drinks and waited for Costello to talk. Before long he accommodated us.

After filling Felicity in on what we found in the desert, he began.

"What I am about to tell you is part fact and part conjecture. It goes without saying that what I tell you never leaves this room."

Felicity and I both nodded in agreement.

Costello continued. "In the mid-seventies, a prominent former union leader disappeared. I won't mention any names since this is an ongoing investigation, but if you read the newspapers back then or caught the national news on TV, you came across this man's name. It was always assumed that this union leader had been involved with organized crime elements. In fact, he spent a few years in jail on corruption charges. When he got out there was concern in certain quarters he would try to reassert his control of the union.

"One morning in 1975, he walked out the front door of his house and went to a restaurant in Detroit to meet some people. When they did not show up, he walked to a pay phone across the street and called his wife. After that, he was never seen again. All of this may be familiar to you.

"At the time of the disappearance, there was a diner in Secaucus, New Jersey, named Frankie's Place, run by a fellow by the name of Frankie Bellini. Frankie, who was called Frankie the Stick because of his thin appearance and twig-like arms and legs, was long rumored to be connected to the mob and was even suspected of being a Mafia hit man. At the time of the union leader's disappearance, Frankie the Stick was questioned by the authorities based on an anonymous tip, but they found nothing and turned their attentions elsewhere.

"Shortly thereafter, Frankie packed up his belongings and took his diner and headed out west. That's where the story ends...until a few months ago, when the bureau got another anonymous tip that Frankie the Stick Bellini was responsible for the death of the union leader and was living in a small town in the middle of the California desert. The bureau has received thousands of tips since the man's disappearance and tries to follow up on any credible information. I was assigned to check into this one.

"That's the factual part of the story. The rest is pure speculation on my part, but I think it is an accurate depiction. I can't prove it, and it may never be proven. In fact, I hope it never is proven.

"Here's what I think," Costello continued.

Before he could go any further, Felicity raised her left hand with a signal for him to stop talking. Costello obliged.

Felicity had drunk about half her glass of ginger ale. Without saying a word, she reached toward the tray, grabbed the bottle of Old Grand-Dad, and filled her glass to the top. She took a good-sized sip followed by a slight shiver and said to Costello, "Continue."

Before he went on, Costello and I also took the opportunity to refresh our glasses.

"Here's what I think," he continued where he had left off. "Frankie the Stick was somehow involved in the murder of the union leader, either as murderer or accomplice. From what I have learned during the investigation, I don't think Frankie had the disposition or the personality to be the hit man, although I could be mistaken. He was involved with illegal activities, run from his diner, but just making book and running numbers.

"A likelier scenario is that someone else murdered the union boss and that the obsolete water tank sitting behind Frankie's Place was a convenient place to deposit the body, either temporarily or permanently.

"Frankie was aware that the body was stashed in his tank. At some point, he decided it was best not to continue to reside in New Jersey. Whether he was spooked by the visit from the police or he was concerned that the mob would like as few living witnesses as possible to the victim's whereabouts, or both, I'm not sure. In any event, he took off, diner, water tank, and all, looking for a place in the middle of nowhere where no one would ever look for him."

"That place being Cordoba," I interjected.

"Exactly," said Costello. He turned to Felicity. "No offense, Felicity, but not many people would stop here, and fewer would choose to linger."

"I guess they don't know what they are missing," said Felicity, offended despite Costello's instructions. The bourbon was making her feisty.

"I agree with you wholeheartedly," Costello responded. "After spending an extended time here, I realize how special this place is, but for the first few days, all I could think of was the fastest way to get out of town. I'll wager the sheriff here had the same reaction."

"Something like that," I said, taking a quick drink, amazed at the accuracy of his observations. "But I'm not the sheriff anymore."

"That's good," Costello said. "We want as little involvement with the law as possible. Any questions so far?"

"Why didn't Frank—Frankie leave the tank and the body back in New Jersey?" asked Felicity.

"A diner with a water tank out back is an ordinary sight, but a solitary tank sitting in the road would invite attention. He could have dumped it somewhere, but in either event, it might be traced back to him, and he couldn't take that chance.

"Well, I guess it's obvious at this point that Frankie the Stick Bellini moved his diner to Cordoba and changed his name to Frank Blaine. Along the way, he also decided to adopt the persona of Hilda Bluff as a disguise, in case someone was following him. So, he picked up the padding and wig and makeup and kept traveling west until he hit Cordoba."

"Why the double identity? Why not just become Hilda?" I asked.

"I have no idea," Costello said. "Maybe he figured it would be too hard to disguise himself as a woman forever. Perhaps he wanted to establish the identities of both Frank and Hilda so that after the heat wore off and he felt safe, Hilda could conveniently leave town and just Frank would remain.

"As for the split in the personalities, you'd have to talk to a psychiatrist. I have no doubts that Frank and Hilda are two different people now. Take for example the talking and arguing the Flagg sisters hear. I don't know when it happened or why. Maybe the desert heat got to Frank, or he needed someone to confide in about the crime and the only one he could trust was Hilda. But at some point, the two became separate personalities.

"Anyway, to finish up the story, I arrived in town a couple of weeks ago and checked out the diner. The Flagg sisters saw me one night, searching around the back of the diner. Frank, or the part of him that was still Frankie, got worried that the past was catching up with him and decided he better do something. Early one morning before it got light, he went to the tank and loaded up the bones and clothing in an old potato sack, threw them in his pickup, and drove out to the desert to bury them. The Flagg sisters also saw that, not that they were snooping."

"Hilda also told me she saw Frank that morning," I added. "I guess you're right about the split personalities."

Costello nodded. "She told me the same story. Frank buried the bones and the clothes in two separate holes up on that little hill. There the story would have ended except Frank buried the bones too close to the edge of the hill. A couple of nights later, we got that heavy downpour that washed the dirt and the bones down to the bottom of the hill, where they were later discovered by Lucky and the Kid.

"And that's where it now stands," Costello concluded.

Felicity and I looked at each other in slight disbelief, and neither of us spoke for a few minutes before I said to Costello, "So that body out in the desert is who I think it is?"

"It could be, but then again, it could be someone else. There was a lot of mob activity in that area at the time. It could just as easily be some other fellow who got on the wrong side of the wrong people. The identity could be confirmed by DNA testing and dental records, but that's not going to happen."

Felicity and I looked at each other again. This time it was Felicity who spoke. "What do you mean it's not going to happen?"

"If I reported this and the bureau investigated and found out this is who I think it is, what would happen? Frank would be picked up, questioned, and arrested. I don't think I want that to happen. If Frankie was involved in the killing, and as I said that's unlikely but possible, you can't pin the blame on Frank or Hilda. At this point, I don't even think Frankie exists anymore. At best, it's five percent Frankie, forty-five percent Frank, and fifty percent Hilda.

"Even if Frank was found incompetent, once they found out about Hilda, he would be put away somewhere where Frank, and definitely Hilda, don't deserve to be.

"And even if Frank gets off, do you want this town crawling with reporters and TV people? What would that do to Frank and Hilda? Do you want to see the Flagg sisters interviewed on national television? Do the other citizens of Cordoba need to have their lives pried into and made public?

"No, sir," he concluded, "I couldn't live with myself if I did something like that."

"You're right on the effects the publicity would have on Cordoba, and I think you are doing the right thing by not reporting it," said Felicity, "but won't you get in trouble if someone finds out?"

"Trouble is a mild word for what I'll be in if this is discovered. But hopefully, it won't be. The only people who know that body is out there are Lucky, the Kid, and the three of us. Now, Lucky and the Kid may say something around town, but no one will think anything of it. Just another body out in the desert. They call this area Death Valley for a reason."

"That's why you had Lucky burn the clothes," I said.

"Yes," responded Costello. "So Lucky knows a little more than I would like, but I'm not worried about him. That leaves the three of us. Obviously, I'm not going to incriminate myself, which just leaves the two of you. You could get some kind of reward and maybe a book deal if you went to the authorities, but somehow I'm not worried."

"You know the secret is safe with us," Felicity said. "But why tell us in the first place?"

"Well, Milo already knew part of the story. I guess I wanted someone else to know. Sort of like Frank maybe confiding in Hilda. I didn't want to be the only one keeping this secret inside. Besides, it's a heck of a story and I wanted to tell it to someone."

"What happens next?" I said.

"I wrap up the investigation and report that this was nothing but another false lead."

"What were you doing the two days you were away?" Felicity asked. "Checking out more leads?"

"No, like I said, I went to Las Vegas for a little downtime, partly at the bureau's expense, although 'I Love Lucy' finished first and paid for part of the cost," he said, giving me a wink.

"I guess you'll be leaving town soon, now that your work is done," I said.

"I'm checking out tomorrow," he replied. "I may take a little detour through Las Vegas on my way back. But I've become somewhat attached to Cordoba and your wonderful hospitality, Felicity, to say nothing about your cooking. Don't be surprised to see me back here some time, this time on vacation."

"Thank you," said Felicity, "you're welcome anytime." Then turning to me she said, "I guess that means you'll be leaving too?"

"Yes," I replied, "I should get back to San Diego to check in," knowing full well there was nothing of importance to return for. "But since this is my last night," I said to Felicity, "why not let me take you out to dinner? You deserve a night off after cooking for us every night."

"Are you asking me out on a date?" she asked, brightening up a little.

"Yes, I guess I am," I replied.

"That would be nice," she said, then hesitated, "but I have to think of the other guests."

"Don't give it a second thought," said Costello. "The three of us can manage on our own. I'm a good cook myself and can whip up something for dinner. My going-away present for you."

"In that case, I accept your offer, Milo," Felicity said. "Since it is still early in the day, I think I'll take a little nap and let the effects of the bourbon and the conversation wear off some."

"Sounds good," I said. "I have a few errands I want to run before tonight."

Felicity went upstairs for her nap, dropping the tray of drinks off in the kitchen on her way.

Costello got up and pulled the two buttons out of his jacket pocket. He handed one to me and said, "Now we both have a souvenir."

CHAPTER 36

A LITTLE OFF THE TOP

My first stop was Indian Charlie's cactus ranch. I was planning on leaving early the next morning and wanted to say good-bye to Charlie. When I drove up, he was out in the fields tending the cacti. He had dug a line of irrigation ditches around the cacti and was busy watering with a hose attached to a water spigot about fifty feet away.

As he twisted and turned the hose, a large German shepherd ran over and took a bite out of the hose.

"Leave the hose alone, Fritz," he screamed at the dog. "It's got enough holes in it already."

When I got closer, I saw that there were several small holes in the hose, all squirting little sprays of water at varying distances from the nozzle. As a result, the flow coming from the nozzle was weak.

"Why don't you just lay the hose down next to the ditch," I hollered. "With all those holes, you could water the whole field without moving."

Indian Charlie laughed and motioned toward the dog. "That's Fritzie's fault. But these don't need much water and don't need extensive care. They sort of grow on their own. I have to keep busy somehow."

"How's Herodotus coming along?" I asked, mentioning the book he borrowed from Felicity.

"He's in Egypt right now. He seems to have been everywhere and seen everything and loved to gossip. I should be done with it soon. I don't want to upset Felicity by keeping it too long."

"I'm sure she doesn't mind," I replied.

"She doesn't," Charlie said. "She's quite a woman, as I'm sure you noticed."

"I have noticed," I said. "In fact, I'm having dinner with her to-night."

"That's nice," said Indian Charlie, "and you seem like a nice guy, Milo, but you're just passing through and Felicity has been hurt before, so I hope you won't do anything you shouldn't."

"Don't worry, Charlie," I said. "I've grown fond of her and wouldn't do anything to hurt her."

"Didn't think you would," said Charlie, "and I don't mean to sound like an overprotective father. But this is a close-knit town, and we believe in looking after each other. Sometimes we overdo it a little. I even thought of making a play for Felicity at one time, but I like the solitary life out here in the desert, and I knew that wasn't for her."

"We're just having a quiet dinner since I'll be leaving tomorrow. That's why I came by. I wanted to say good-bye. And while I'm here I'd like to buy a little souvenir."

"Sure." Charlie laid down the hose and walked over to his pickup. He pulled out a cactus in a little pot and handed it to me. "No charge," he added. "Drop by again soon."

"I will. I have a feeling I'll be back this way sometime soon."

"Have a safe trip back to San Diego, and watch your step on the way out," Indian Charlie said as I turned to leave.

"Will do," I replied. "I don't want to end up in Doc's office having cactus spines removed from my feet."

"I was talking about Fritzie," Charlie said. "He likes to relieve himself among the plants. Not much Doc can do about that. But be careful around the cactus too."

I negotiated the dangers presented by Indian Charlie's fields and headed back to town. I had another destination in mind.

My hair was a little shaggy and wanted to get a haircut if possible before my date. On my travels around Cordoba, I had noticed an old-fashioned barber pole on First Street just off Main Street. I figured that the store was either a barbershop or an antique store that had an old barber's pole outside for display. As I pulled up, I discovered that it was indeed a barbershop as the lettering on the front window verified: "Monte's Barbershop."

The barber's pole in front of the building was still in working order as the red- and the white-striped pole was slowly rotating.

When I first looked at the rotating pole, it reminded me of a child swirling a candy cane around in her mouth. But after staring at it for a minute, a sort of hypnotic effect took over and I felt like Jimmy Stewart when he was falling in *Vertigo*. I quickly shook off the effects and entered the building, which was an old wooden, one- story, standalone building that looked like it had been around since the 1800s.

The entrance was in the center of the building, and to each side, there were windows that protruded a little bit on each side, like bay windows. There was a shelf inside the alcove on both sides piled with magazines that were not quite of the vintage of Doc's collection but were far from current. One look at the condition of the magazines and I knew that Monte was not a collector like Doc was.

Beside the alcoves on both sides were several straight-backed wooden chairs. The floor was wood with no carpeting or covering. The walls in the back of the shop and to the right were covered with pages that had been cut from issues of *National Geographic* showing scenery and wildlife from around the globe.

The wall on the left was covered by a large mirror with a shelf below, which held various barber's utensils. In the middle of the room to the left and facing the mirror were two ancient objects. The first was an ornate barber's chair that looked like it had been serving customers since the days of Wyatt Earp.

The second object was an old gentleman seated in the barber chair reading a magazine. He turned as I entered and climbed down from the chair.

"Howdy," he said. "Need a haircut?"

He was a rather frail-looking old man who was stooped over. He wore black pants and a short white coat, the kind that doctors and barbers wear. On his head was a battered blue baseball cap with an emblem on the front I recognized as the "B" of the Brooklyn Dodgers. Bushy gray sideburns protruded from under the cap, matched by a pair of bushy eyebrows. His nose was thin, and his face was wrinkled, but his eyes were alert and he looked like he knew what was going on.

His only other significant features were the two large hands that were shaking uncontrollably. It looked like he had long since stopped trying to hide the shakes.

My mind took him in, and I realized that those were not the hands I wanted working in close proximity to my head with sharp scissors, so I made small talk while trying to come up with a way to make a graceful exit.

"You must be Monte," I stuttered.

"Well, sir, I am and I ain't," he said. His sharp eyes had caught my glance at his hands and my reluctance to enter. "Come in and I'll tell you the story," he said. Holding his hands up, he assured me, "Don't worry about these. I can't do a thing with them except when I cut hair. Then they are steady as a rock. Darndest thing. Can't figure it out. Come in. Come in."

Seeing no way to make a graceful exit, I walked in. Monte took me by the arm and guided me to the barber's chair, giving my arm a nice massage with his trembling hand. At this point, I was just hoping to avoid bloodshed and leave with a haircut that wouldn't cause Felicity to cancel our date in embarrassment. But a part of me was intrigued by his comment about his name. It looked like he had a story to tell and I wanted to hear it.

"You must be the new fellow in town," he said as he seated me in the chair.

"Yes, my name is Milo Forbes."

"Friend of Ben's, I hear." He talked in short, clipped sentences and had a certain cadence that made you think he was reciting poetry. "Been here several days," he said, more a comment than a question.

He wrapped a paper band around my neck, covered me with a sheet, and shakily grabbed a pair of scissors and a comb from the shelf below the mirror. There was no sign of clippers or any electric grooming devices—just several pairs of scissors, several combs floating like medical specimens in a jar full of blue liquid, a straight razor and shaving cup and brush, and several bottles of lotions and potions covered in dust.

"How do you want it cut?" he asked, surveying my shaggy salt-and-pepper hair.

"Just cut the white ones and leave the black ones," I said to ease the tension, mine, not his. I wanted to add, "And leave the ears," but didn't.

He laughed and said, "I'll do my best."

He raised the scissors and comb to my head, and as he had told me, when he began to cut, his hands became steady and he cut with precision and speed, the scissors making a quick clip, clip, clip sound almost like someone typing on a typewriter.

After he got settled into his routine—and I relaxed a little—Monte began his story, his speech as clipped and controlled as the action of the scissors.

"As I told you, Monte is my name and it ain't. I was born Stanley Loomis many years ago in Orange, New Jersey. Stone's throw from Newark. Uneventful childhood. Indifferent student. My only real passion was baseball," he said, deciding to throw in a complete sentence for novelty.

"Dodger fan?" I asked, motioning to the baseball cap he wore.

"Brooklyn fan," he scolded me. "Back then we had three teams in New York, all of them good. Every World Series champ from forty-nine to fifty-six. Three games on television every night—Yankees, Giants, Dodgers. Have to be strong up the middle to win. Well, sir, those teams had three Hall of Fame center fielders. Two Hall of Fame shortstops. Two Hall of Fame catchers. A Hall of Fame second baseman.

"My team was the Dodgers. Hated the Yankees. Hated the Giants more. Second worst day of my life, October 3, 1951. Shot heard round the world. Best day of my life, game seven, 1955 World Series. Dodgers beat the Yankees. Only Brooklyn title.

"Worst year of my life, 1957. Dodgers and Giants move to the West Coast."

He continued as he worked his way around my head. "Well, sir, I was a young man in 1957. Had a small barbershop in Orange. Decent living. I sold my shop and follow the Dodgers out to LA. I was single, so no strings. Bought an old used car. Drove out west.

"Well, sir, when I got out to LA and saw the Dodgers of 1958, I knew I had made a mistake. No Ebbets Field. Playing in a football stadium. Hundred feet to the left-field stands, six hundred to center. And the team. Jackie was gone. Retired after he was traded to the Giants. Refused to play for the Giants. Campy paralyzed in a car crash in December of fifty-seven. Pee Wee was too old and Koufax was too young. Hodges ended up with the Mets. Snider played for the Giants and the Mets.

"I realized that it wasn't the same team, and Los Angeles wasn't Brooklyn. Snider was the Duke of Flatbush, not the Duke of Hollywood. Raised in California and returned after his baseball days. Had an avocado ranch. But he belonged to Brooklyn. Always has, always will."

By now he was done with my hair. He spun me around to look in the mirror and held a hand mirror at the back of my head so I could get a full view. Although it was difficult to see the back since his hands had begun shaking again since he had stopped cutting, it was obvious he had done a first-rate job.

"What do you think?" he asked.

"Very nice," I said.

"Now for a shave," he said. "Gotta be clean-shaven for your date." I have no idea how he knew about the date. I guess news travels fast in a small town.

Monte pumped a lever on the old chair until I was almost prone. Surprisingly, I wasn't concerned as Monte's shaking hands poured a little hot water in the shaving mug and worked up a lather with the brush. I wasn't even worried as he lathered my face, picked up the straight razor with a trembling right hand, and sharpened it on a leather strap attached to the chair. He had done a good job with the hair and I needed a shave. Besides, I hadn't yet heard the full story.

Monte's hands steadied again as he shaved my face. He proceeded so lightly I felt nothing but a slight enjoyable tickle. Every few strokes he flicked the lather off the razor into the sink in front of him. As he shaved, he continued his story.

"Well, sir, after a few months in California, I decided I'd had enough. Got into my car and headed back to New Jersey. Took the southern route. That old car developed engine troubles on Route 8. Cordoba was the closest town, so I headed here.

"Well, sir, I had no money and I couldn't afford to fix the car. Sold it for scrap. Needed to make money. Went looking for a job. Found this old barbershop that had been vacant for years. Asked if I could buy or rent it. No one in town could quite recall who owned the building, so they told me if I clean it up, it's mine.

"I cleaned her up and moved in, living in the back. As I said, I was a little low on cash, so I couldn't afford to change the name painted on the window from Monte to Stanley. Left it the way it was. By the time I had enough money to replace the name, everyone in town was already calling me Monte. Didn't want to confuse them any more than necessary, so I started answering to Monte.

"That's all there is, except I haven't left this town or watched a baseball game since."

Monte then became silent. He had reached the end of his story.

"Do the people in town now know your real name is Stanley?" I asked.

"Half do, half don't," Monte replied. "But they all call me Monte, and that's what I answer to."

He was now finished with the shave and returned me to an upright position. He added lather to the sides and back of my head and trimmed those areas with the razor, then took a hot towel out of a little heated cabinet below the sink, held it to my face for a moment, and used it to remove the leftover lather.

He grabbed a bottle on the counter that contained a light blue liquid, shook a little on his hands, rubbed it between his hands and then applied it to my face. It had a slight medicinal smell and did not burn as I expected—rather, it felt cool and refreshing.

His last acts were to remove the sheet and tissue paper, dust around the back of my head with a soft brush, then brush any remaining hair off with a whisk broom.

I got out of the chair and admired myself in the mirror. The haircut and shave were an improvement, and I looked halfway decent for a middle-aged man who had forgotten how to take care of himself.

"That'll be two dollars," Monte said. "Inflation, you know."

I handed him a five and told him to keep the change.

"Much obliged," he said and threw the bill in a drawer beneath the shelf. "Maybe now I can afford to change the name on the window. Think I'll change it to Gus just to have a little fun." He laughed and winked.

"Thanks a lot, Monte or Stanley or Gus," I said. "I enjoyed your story."

Monte was now cleaning up the clippings from the floor using a broom and dustpan with handles long enough, so he didn't have to bend over. It looked like this would be an all-day project since any hair his shaky right hand swept into the dustpan was immediately shaken back out by his left.

"Well, sir," he said, "come back again and I'll tell you about my road trip across the country. Say hello to Miss Felicity for me."

I assured him I would do both—and I meant it.

CHAPTER 37

AN EVENING AT JIMMY CHANG'S

I went back to the boardinghouse to get ready for the evening's date. I found an iron and ironing board in a closet in the upstairs hall and removed some of the wrinkles from the suit I was wearing the day I arrived in Cordoba. I then decided to clean up a little bit and walked down the hall toward the bath. All the rooms were quiet on both sides, so the other boarders were out or napping. I walked down to Felicity's room and heard her moving around, her nap over.

I knocked on the door and said, "I'm going to take a quick bath. Will you be needing the bathroom?"

"No, I'm finished with it," she replied. "And take your time. It takes me a little longer than usual these days to get made up."

"Don't worry. You look great without the makeup."

I took a relaxing bath and went back to my room to get dressed. I surveyed myself in the mirror and was not disgusted with the results. I was outfitted in a black suit, white shirt, blue-and black striped tie, and a fresh haircut, which somehow gave me the illusion of respectability.

Felicity was still in her room when I went downstairs, and the lower floor was still empty, so I went to the parlor to wait. I sat on the sofa and fidgeted, feeling like a schoolboy waiting for his prom date to come down. It had been a while since I had dated a woman.

Before long I heard Felicity's door closing, so I walked out into the hall. She was standing at the top of the stairs looking radiant.

She wore a dress covered with pink and light purple flowers that came to just above her knees and black shoes with medium high heels and straps around the ankles. A knit shawl hung around her shoulders. Her hair was brushed straight with a slight curl at the bottom, with one side brushed back and tied behind her ear with a small ornamental orchid.

As she walked down the stairs, I struggled to get my breath back and blurted, "You look terrific."

"Thanks," she said as she reached the bottom. "You look pretty spiffy yourself."

She reached up and straightened my tie and I caught the scent of her perfume, a combination of citrus and some sort of flower which I couldn't identify since my knowledge of flower aromas is limited. Whatever it was, it smelled great.

"This is for you." I pulled the miniature cactus I got from Indian Charlie from behind my back. "It was the best I could do with the short notice and lack of florists in Cordoba."

"Thank you. That was very thoughtful of you but forgive me if I don't wear it as a corsage," Felicity said, placing the cactus on the stand in the hall. "Let's go in here and decide where we're going." Felicity headed for the parlor. "By the way, your hair looks nice."

"Thanks. Monte says hi."

"He's a nice man," Felicity said. "Did you get the story about his name?"

"Yes, interesting."

"You have to go back and hear it again sometime. He changes some of the details each time. The last time he saw me at the diner, he said he joined up with a traveling circus that went broke near here. He said the owners just took off and let all the wild animals loose in the desert. So look out for runaway lions and giraffes on your way out of town."

"I got the Brooklyn Dodger version."

"I think that is the true story, or mostly true. So where would you like to have dinner? I'm afraid the choices around here are limited. Frank doesn't serve much food at the tavern, and there's no other restaurant in Cordoba. There's Jimmy Chang's Chinese restaurant in Bell City and a few smaller places. There's a Mexican place over in Chiquita, but that's a longer drive."

"Then Jimmy Chang's it is. Chinese food isn't my favorite, but I appreciate a good egg foo young."

"Don't worry, Jimmy's menu is eclectic," Felicity said as we left the house. I held the car door for her, and we headed for Bell City.

Bell City has a wide paved Main Street with diagonal parking spaces on both sides. Following Felicity's instructions, I found a parking space in front of Jimmy Chang's.

The restaurant was in a wide brick building that looked like it had been two side-by-side businesses that had been converted into one. There were entrances in front of both former buildings. The one on the right had a sign that said, "Use Other Door," so we headed for the door on the left.

Both buildings were fronted with glass windows, much like Monte's, and on the window to the right of the working entrance, the name of the establishment was painted, although with much more elaborate lettering. After pausing to contemplate whether Jimmy had to change his name to match his window, I stood in front and read the sign before entering.

The lettering was gold, in an oriental-looking script. In large letters, centered in the middle of the window, was the restaurant's name: "Jimmy Chang's Szechuan Palace, Pizzeria and Biergarten." Below in somewhat smaller letters was written, "Entertainment Nightly." To the left of the lettering was a painting of an Asian chef wearing a chef's hat and throwing a round pizza dough in the air. To the right was a picture of a leprechaun, dressed in bright green, jumping in the air and clicking his heels together while holding a mug of beer.

Since at this point, nothing in the area could surprise me much, I gave Felicity a slightly quizzical look.

"I told you the menu was eclectic, didn't I?" She smiled.

I turned back and looked past the lettering into the building, but this looked like a normal Chinese restaurant. Seeing nothing further of interest, I took Felicity's elbow and we headed inside.

There was a long bar that ran the length of the building, and tables lined the wall to the right, interrupted by a couple of doors. The tables had white tablecloths topped by small bowls of fortune cookies.

To the right of the entrance was a glass counter holding a cash register and the usual assortment of mints and toothpicks. A rosy-faced girl of high school age stood behind the counter, ringing up departing customers.

To the left was a podium, about five feet high, behind which, I saw with some difficulty, stood an Asian gentleman, also about five feet high, straining on tiptoes to see the reservation schedule on the podium. When he saw us enter, he scurried around the podium and said, "Howdy doody, Missy Felicity, how you tonight?"

"Hello, Jimmy, I'm fine," she responded. "Jimmy, this is my friend Milo Forbes. He's visiting from San Diego."

"Howdy doody, Mr. Forbes."

"Hello, Jimmy." Scanning the restaurant, which was quite full, I added, "Looks like business is pretty good."

"We do okay. Friday night always busy." Then turning to Felicity, "Where you sit tonight?"

"It's a beautiful night, Jimmy. Do you have any tables available in the garden?"

"Always for you, there is a table." Jimmy grabbed menus from a slot in the side of the podium and said, "Follow me."

We followed him to the first door on the wall to the right and walked through to the other building. The stereo system was playing Dean Martin singing "That's Amore," and the atmosphere changed from Chinese to Italian. The layout was about the same except there was no bar and the tables were covered with red and white checked tablecloths. The aroma also changed as Italian dishes were being served.

After taking a few steps into the Italian zone, Jimmy turned left and headed toward the back of the building. We followed him through a door in the back onto a patio that went back about twenty yards and covered the length of both buildings. There were more tables scattered around, this time wooden with no tablecloths. The patio was surrounded by a wooden latticework fence about six feet tall, and the sides of the patio were lined with large plastic potted plants to give the area a feeling of seclusion. The floor of the patio was composed of wooden slats.

Jimmy guided us to a table against the building's wall and about halfway down. There were few tables in this area and potted plants on both sides, which provided us with privacy.

Jimmy dropped the menus on the table and said, "Waitress be here soon." He smiled and left.

Felicity mercifully did not say anything but gave me a little more time to take in my surroundings.

My attention was focused on the far end of the patio. Upon a stage in the middle of the area, a German oompah band was playing "Let Me Call You Sweetheart."

The band was four men dressed in white shirts and short black pants held up by wide suspenders covered in embroidered patterns and wearing Tyrolean hats. To the left of the band, a barbershop quartet, wearing white shirts with vertical red stripes and straw boaters, crooned the words to the song. An elevated wooden bandstand was in front of the band. The bandstand was occupied by a few couples trying to keep time.

Other than that, there was nothing unusual about the patio except for the tiki bar tucked away in the far left-hand corner. A bartender wearing a lei was engaged in serving a couple some drinks in hollowed-out coconuts with little parasols peeking out.

Felicity spoke. "Well, what do you think of Jimmy's?"

"It certainly is different."

"We don't have many restaurants in the area, so Jimmy tries to cover all the bases."

The waitress arrived, another fresh-faced teenager in a Bavarian costume. "Hi, Miss Fremont," she said to Felicity. "Are you ready to order or do you need more time?"

Noting I would obviously need more time to recover and study the menu, Felicity responded, "Thanks, Jennie, I think we'll need some time."

"No problem. Would you like to order drinks?"

"I'll have a red wine. Milo?"

"I'll have a mug of the German beer," I said, surveying the drink list on the menu. There was a notice at the bottom informing diners, "Happy hour 5:00 to 7:00 every night except Sunday through Thursday."

"You got it," said Jennie. "I'll be right back."

As Jennie left, I again surveyed the scene in front of me, and my eyes were directed to another waitress, also in Bavarian garb, waiting on a table on the far side of the patio.

"Isn't that Annie Webster?" I asked Felicity, pointing in that direction.

"Yes, she works here," Annie said with a surprised look on her face. "I'm surprised to see her back to work so soon."

"Me too. Maybe she wants to return to her normal routine and get her mind off Billy."

After another short period of silence, Felicity said, "I guess we should get the obvious topic out of the way first so we can enjoy the rest of the evening. What do you think of Mr. Costello's story?"

"I can't be sure, but it makes sense. And I think his decision to keep his findings a secret is the right course of action. I can't picture the citizens of Cordoba being put under a media spotlight."

Felicity agreed and we discussed a few parts of Costello's story for a few minutes, but we were both anxious to put the conversation behind us by the time Jennie returned with our drinks. She laid them on the table along with a small platter of German-style soft pretzels. "Need more time?" she asked, noticing that our menus had not been touched.

"If you don't mind, Jennie, I think we'll wait a while before ordering," Felicity said. "We'll just sit here and enjoy the evening."

"Super," Jennie replied. "Just give me a holler when you're ready."

It was a perfect evening to enjoy. The desert temperature had dropped as the sun was setting, not uncomfortable but cool to where Felicity was pulling the shawl around her and I was glad I had a jacket on. The blue sky was darkening as night approached but still contained swirls of pink cotton candy clouds. Felicity looked beautiful and I wondered why she was still single.

Felicity took a sip of her wine and I tasted my beer. The German beer tasted suspiciously like Frank's Fromova, but again, it was cold and tasted fine. Small chips of ice floated on top of the beer, and my fingerprints were visible on the frosted mug when I put it down.

Felicity took a pretzel from the platter. "Jimmy's idea of complimentary breadsticks," she said.

I followed suit and grabbed a pretzel. It was a small version of a soft German pretzel, still hot and lightly salted. As I bit into it, I discovered it was soft on the inside and had a nice crunch on the outside.

"Very good," I said. "This is quite a place Jimmy's got here."

After we had sat for a few minutes, enjoying the drinks and the pretzels and the weather, Felicity said, "Aren't you going to ask me the question?"

"What question?" I responded, confused.

"The question I always seem to get asked when I meet someone new. How come a nice girl like you isn't married?"

"I wasn't..." I stammered.

"It's all right. I'm used to it. You know, to begin with, you are aware by now that there aren't many eligible bachelors in Cordoba, and the few unmarried men, like Ben, are determined to stay that way."

I started to say something, but Felicity quickly continued. "Of course, some eligible men stay at the boardinghouse, mostly traveling salesmen and campers on the way to the desert." She then added, "And the occasional private detective," looking at me and smiling.

"I've had a few relationships in the past," she continued, "but most of the men were not interested in settling down, except maybe in the dining room and the bedroom. Even the ones who stayed on never lasted longer than a few weeks without getting bored with our small town—and me, I guess—and moving on."

She again looked at me and gave me another slight smile. "That's my story. What about you? There must be plenty of eligible ladies in San Diego. How come none of them have hooked you? Or has one?"

"Nope," I said, "no attachments and never been married. I'd like to say that in my dangerous line of business, there's no room for relationships. I'd like to say that, but unfortunately, I can't. The business I get isn't dangerous. I simply haven't met anyone who has made me feel like I want to spend the rest of my life with them. And the few possibilities didn't want to spend their lives with me. Similar to your experiences, many leave town after a few weeks of dating me, and these are lifelong residents of San Diego."

Felicity laughed and I continued, "The only people I know in San Diego are my secretary and my accountant, neither of whom I need, and a few bartenders that I do need. I have a few friends, mostly married, who provide dinner and consolation."

"Then why stay there?" Felicity asked.

I started to answer but couldn't think of a reason, so I picked up a menu and said, "Why don't we order. I'm starting to work up an appetite."

Felicity smiled again and picked up her menu.

The menu was large and covered in brown plastic to simulate leather. Inside were seven or eight laminated pages printed on both sides, arranged by style of cooking, with a separate page each for Chinese, Italian, and German selections. There was also a page with items that did not fit into the three categories, with everything from meatloaf to corned beef and cabbage to tamales.

"If you want something that's not on the menu, ask for it and they can whip it up in the kitchen," Felicity said. I replied that that would not be necessary.

Felicity decided on a garden salad and the Chinese beef and broccoli. I opted for the day's special from the German page, a sample of German sausages titled "From Best to Wurst." We motioned to Jennie, who had been busy waiting on other tables while keeping one eye trained on our table. She came over and took our orders, which included a couple more drinks. While we were waiting, we listened to the band, accompanied by the quartet, playing hits from the turn of the century, the twentieth, not the twenty-first. There were a few couples on the floor dancing, including ladies who couldn't get their husbands to join them.

The band was playing "The Sidewalks of New York" when our food showed up. My sausages were accompanied by a side dish of spaetzle, and both were delicious. Felicity seemed to be enjoying her meal also and there was little talk during dinner.

When we had finished, Jennie showed up again and took our plates. We declined dessert but opted for coffee. Jennie left but quickly returned with a stainless-steel pot of coffee, two cups and sugar, and cream. She filled our cups, then left the pot on the table and left.

The sky was now dark, and the stars shone as we drank our coffee.

As we were engaged in small talk and digesting our meal, Annie, who was serving a nearby table, noticed us and walked over.

She said hello and Felicity asked her, "Are you doing okay, Annie?"

"I'm holding up, trying to keep busy."

"Well, if there's anything you need, just ask," Felicity said.

"Thanks. If you don't mind, Felicity, can I steal your man for a minute?"

"He's not my man, but I'd appreciate it if you return him in one piece," Felicity joked.

Annie looked for a place where we could speak in private and located a few empty barstools at the end of the tiki bar. I followed her over and we took the seats.

"I wanted to thank you for everything you've done for me," Annie began.

"It was nothing," I responded.

"Don't say that. It meant a great deal."

"In that case, I am glad to have been of service."

"I talked to Mr. Church this afternoon."

"How did that go?"

"He told me they were processing my claim and I should receive the money soon. I told him that Billy's death was not an accident but was suicide and I could only take the ten thousand dollars."

This did not surprise me, but I asked Annie, "Didn't Church want some proof?"

"He did. I told him Billy had left me a suicide note. He asked to see it, but I told him I had destroyed it rather than keep a reminder around."

"Did that satisfy him?"

"Not completely, but I told him that, in good conscience, I couldn't accept the hundred thousand dollars and I would return the check if they sent it to me. That seemed to settle things for him."

"You could have done a lot of things with that money," I said.

"Maybe," she responded, "but I can't think of much that I want to do. The ten thousand will pay off the trailer and leave me a little left over to put away for Billy Jr. And I still have my job here."

"I'm proud of you, Annie."

She didn't respond but sat for a few minutes with a faraway look in her eyes.

Finally, she said, "Jim came to see me last night."

I didn't say anything, so she continued. "I saw him at the funeral. He was standing way in the back so no one would see him. He came over to see me last night after you and everyone else had left. I think he was watching the house and waiting."

"What did he have to say?"

"He was very upset the way things ended with Billy and him. He meant to talk to Billy and me over the years but was too stubborn to do it. Billy's death hit him hard."

"What did you say?"

"I told him we were all at fault and not to blame himself. We both had a good cry." Another silence followed and then, "We might start seeing each other again, you know, take it slowly and see what happens."

I didn't respond, so Annie asked me, "What do you think, Milo? Is that a stupid thing to do?"

"I can't answer that," I replied, "but what I can tell you is that, knowing you, I have every confidence you will make the right decision."

"Thanks again," Annie said. We both stood up and Annie gave me a hug before going back to work. I returned to my table.

"Looks like I have competition," Felicity said, noting the hug.

"No, you're safe," I said. "But it would be nice if you could check in on Annie to see how she's doing. I think she could use a friend to talk to from time to time."

"I was already planning on doing that, but it was nice of you to ask."

I was about to sit down when the band started playing "The Band Played On," and I impulsively said to Felicity, "How about a dance?"

"I'm not the greatest dancer, but I'll give it a shot if you will," she said.

We walked over and stepped onto the dance floor among a few other couples. I hadn't bothered mentioning that I had never been on a dance floor in my life, but Felicity quickly learned this, and gently guided me around the floor. My main concern was holding Felicity and taking in the feel of her body close to mine and the scent of her perfume. As the quartet sang, "Casey would waltz with the strawberry blonde, and the band played on," we danced with our heads close together and my head touching her strawberry blonde hair.

When the song ended, Felicity decided not to press her luck and risk bodily harm by attempting another dance, and she led me back to our seats. It was getting late, so we finished our coffee and retraced our steps through the biergarten, the Italian restaurant, and the Chinese restaurant.

"How everything?" Jimmy asked Felicity as I paid the bill.

"Everything was wonderful, as usual," Felicity said.

I grabbed a mint and studied the souvenirs in the display case below the counter. I considered buying a bright green T-shirt with lettering on the front that said, "I ate at Jimmy Chang's and lived to tell about it," but Felicity noticed my interest and dragged me out onto the street.

Jimmy hollered as we were leaving, "You come back soon, hear!"

Felicity dominated the conversation on the way back to Cordoba with stories about the town and its residents. When we arrived at the boardinghouse, she made a quick inspection of the dining room and kitchen and finding that Costello had cleaned up and left everything in order, we climbed the stairs holding hands. I made another attempt to follow Felicity to her room but was once again turned away and pointed toward my room. This time I got a slight kiss on the lips, so I guess I was making progress.

CHAPTER 38

OUT OF CORDOBA

The next morning, I awoke early, got out of bed, and went to the bathroom to wash up and brush my teeth. I returned to my room and packed my clothes and other belongings I had bought in Bell City into their original plastic sales bags. I straightened up the room a little bit and headed downstairs, carrying the bags.

There were suitcases sitting in the hallway by the front door which I assumed belonged to Costello. I started to place my bags next to them, looked at my luggage as compared to his, and stashed my bags around the door to the parlor and out of sight.

I walked into the dining room, where everyone was already seated and digging into a breakfast of eggs, bacon, and rye toast. I said my hellos and dug in myself.

"I guess you are losing a few boarders, Felicity," Costello said between bites. "Forbes and I are ready to go, and Silas said he would be moving on in a few days."

"Yes, it will be a little lonely in this big house," replied Felicity, "but I still have you, Fred, don't I?"

Fred shook his head in agreement. "I'm not going anywhere, except over to Mrs. C's to work on her roof. And I better be getting over there."

He got up and shook hands with Costello and walked around the table and grabbed my hand. "Milo, it's been a pleasure. Hope to see you around here again sometime soon."

"I'm sure I'll be back, Fred. Take care of yourself."

Silas then rose and said, "I'll walk with you over to Mrs. C's, Kid. I have work to do on her roof too."

He also shook hands with Costello and me, and he and Fred went out the door.

When the three of us who remained were finished eating, Costello said, "Well, I guess it's time for me to say good-bye. I've got a lot of driving to do today. And Las Vegas beckons."

He got up and walked into the hall, with Felicity and I following. Before he picked up his bags, he hugged Felicity and shook my hand. On his way out the door, he turned and said, "And remember, our conversation of yesterday should not be repeated."

"What conversation?" I replied. Costello smiled, headed for his car, and drove away.

I helped Felicity with the dishes one last time. We talked a little bit about the previous night's date, and Felicity mentioned how lonely the boardinghouse would be with just about everyone gone.

"I'm sure you'll get a new batch of visitors," I said.

"Yes, there are always people passing through. But I'd prefer a little repeat business," she said, looking at me.

After the dishes were done, I told Felicity I was going to take a quick walk around town and say my good-byes. I asked her if she wanted to join me, but she declined, saying she wanted to do some reading and thinking.

I went out into another hot, sunny desert day and turned down Elm Street to the Flagg sisters' house. They were sitting on their usual perch. Since it was still early in the day, the lemonade had just been made and the glass pitcher was filled with ice cubes that hadn't yet melted. I stayed a short time while Ruth told me about her regrets about wearing that red dress and helping the FBI catch Dillinger. I said my good-byes and continued.

"Come back soon, young man," said Ruth.

"Soon," repeated Mabel.

"Soon," said Jewel.

I have never visited the Grand Canyon, but I imagine this is what it would sound like if you hollered over the edge.

I retraced my steps and walked over to Doc's house. There were no patients waiting, so I talked to Leo and Doc for a while, got a big hug and a thank you from Leo and a hearty handshake from Doc, and proceeded over to Mrs. C's. Fred and Silas were both on the roof, Fred repairing the hole and Silas installing a lightning rod. Roy was out on the front lawn, cleaning up some of the remaining debris from the lightning strike.

"Go right in," he yelled as I walked up the path. "No appointment necessary."

I went in and found Mrs. C in her usual spot beside the fire. The magazines were resting on the table beside her chair, and her eyes were half closed.

"Come in, Milo," she said when she saw me. I entered and took a seat by the fire, forgetting the heat. "I was just daydreaming about my past experiences. You know, what with the roller derby and my life in San Francisco, I've led an exciting life. But I think I've been much happier living here with Roy these past years in tiny, dusty Cordoba. I don't think I realized it until the past few days, but there's something to be said for living a quiet, peaceful life with someone you love, surrounded by people who care for you. Do you know what I mean, Milo?"

I smiled. "It's hard not to know where you're going since it's been drummed into my head from almost everyone in town since I arrived."

Mrs. C smiled back. "Not too subtle, are we? Still, there's truth in what we say, and we're only thinking about your well-being."

I thanked Mrs. Cavendish for caring, and she thanked me for my help as she stood and gave me a hug. I walked outside, gave a wave to Roy, and headed back to the boardinghouse.

Felicity was sitting in a chair in the parlor, a book in her lap. She was holding a handkerchief and I suspected she had been crying but couldn't tell for sure.

Her expression changed to a smile when she saw me, and she walked out into the hall.

"Said all your good-byes?" she asked.

"Just about. I'll stop and see Ben on the way out of town."

We stood awkwardly without talking for a minute; then Felicity grew serious and said, "I guess there's no way I can convince you to stay?"

"I'd like to," I replied truthfully, "but I have things to take care of back in San Diego." I couldn't think of any at the moment.

"Then you better get back," she said, turning angry, "but before you go, let me give you three good reasons why you should stay in Cordoba.

"Number one, from what you told me last night, you've made more friends in Cordoba in less than a week than you have in San Diego in all the years you've lived there."

I didn't reply, so she continued. "Number two, you'll have to come back for this." She reached into the drawer in the stand where she had kept Leo's magazines, pulled out a playing card, and placed it face down on the table.

"What's this?" I turned the card over to discover that it was my missing six of hearts.

"You can't play solitaire in San Diego without it, so you might as well bring your deck of cards back here. Besides, I think you'll discover solitaire doesn't compare to a good game of canasta with your new friends."

"Where did you get this?" I asked, startled.

"Hector found it under the seat of your car before it was towed to Bell City."

"Well, you've made some pretty good points."

"And if those aren't enough to keep you here, here's a third reason." She came over, threw her arm around my neck, and kissed me passionately for a long time.

When she was done, she asked, "Well, what about it?"

"Sorry," I said, "but I'm still going back to San Diego."

As a look of disappointment came over her face, I quickly continued. "I have to pick up a change of underwear and my deck of cards to bring back."

The smile returned to her face and she kissed me again. "Which of my three points convinced you?"

I pointed to the playing card on the table. "I really need that card."

Felicity feigned anger and pushed me toward the door. "Get out of here and go back and get your things. I'll put your bags back up in your room."

"Maybe I could get an upgrade to the master suite," I said.

"Don't rush things, cowboy," she said and gave me another push.

As I was walking down the steps, I wondered if I should tell Felicity that she hadn't needed to convince me to stay. I had decided that last night when I was holding her on the dance floor and the band played on. I decided not to tell her.

I jumped into my car and drove down Main Street to the diner, parking in the gravel lot next to it. I guessed that I would find Ben here since it was around lunchtime. Before entering I headed across the street and went into the general store. Sam was standing at the counter reading a magazine. She looked up when the little bell rang.

I walked over to the counter. "I wanted to say good-bye before I left and thank you for your help."

"But you...you can't leave yet," she stammered. "We haven't solved the case of the prowler yet."

"I don't think we'll see any more of him," I assured her.

"I saw Mr. Costello driving away. I'll bet it was him, huh."

"I wouldn't be surprised."

"Maybe we'll never know what he was looking for."

I nodded. "I guess no one will ever know."

"Well, you still don't have to leave," Sam said. "There are other reasons..."

"Save your breath," I cut her off. "I'm coming back."

Sam ran around the counter and hugged me. "Maybe we can work on another case," she said as I left.

"Maybe," I replied.

I headed across the street to the diner and found Ben, Phil, and Hilda in their usual places. As usual, the rest of the diner was empty.

I walked over and sat next to Ben as Hilda placed a cup of coffee in front of me.

"Heading out?" asked Ben.

"Yes. I was just leaving and wanted to stop and say good-bye."

"I don't suppose..."

I cut Ben off. "I've already heard the Chamber of Commerce speech. I'll be returning."

"That's great," said Ben. "Phil and I were just talking. I don't suppose you'd be interested in becoming the permanent town sheriff? The job doesn't pay much, enough to cover room and board and a little extra, but then as you've seen, there's not a lot to spend money on out here.

"We could use a man of your caliber," Ben continued. "The office has been vacant for quite a while since the last sheriff left."

"Why did the last sheriff leave?" I asked.

"Went off to join the Union Army," Phil jumped in. As usual, I couldn't tell whether he was joking or not, but then again, it didn't matter.

"I'll take the job," I replied to Ben, "with one condition. You let me hire a deputy sheriff."

"We hardly have enough money in the budget for one sheriff," Ben protested.

"Not a problem. I know someone who will work for peanuts."

I said my good-byes to Phil, Ben, and Hilda and headed for the door. "I'll be back in a few weeks."

As I left, Rosemary Clooney was singing "Give me the Simple Life" on the jukebox.

"Make that a few days," I corrected myself.

I got in my car and headed out of town. A little way down the road, I pulled over. I opened the glove box and pulled out two souvenirs from my stay in Cordoba—a small brass button and a pearl-handled penknife. I got out of the car, put the button in my pocket, and walked over to the sign welcoming visitors to Cordoba.

Underneath the crossed-out "73" on the sign, I carved the number 74 into the wood.

I got back in the car, drove south until I reached Route 8, and turned right.

ABOUT THE AUTHOR

Steve Laracy's work has appeared in *Clare Literary Magazine, Candlesticks and Daggers: An Anthology of Mixed-Genre Mysteries,* and *Crimson Streets.*